MATT DICKINSON

Killer Storm.

shrine
bell

www.shrinebell.com

Killer Storm
Matt Dickinson

First published in 2017 by Shrine Bell, an imprint of Vertebrate Publishing.

Shrine Bell
Crescent House, 228 Psalter Lane, Sheffield, S11 8UT, UK
www.shrinebell.com

A CIP catalogue record for this book is available from the British Library.

ISBN 978-1-911342-36-6 (Paperback)
ISBN 978-1-911342-37-3 (Ebook)

10 9 8 7 6 5 4 3 2 1

Production by Vertebrate Publishing
www.v-publishing.co.uk

Shrine Bell and Vertebrate Publishing are committed
to printing on paper from sustainable sources.

Printed and bound in Great Britain by Clays Ltd, St Ives plc

To my brother
Paul

CHAPTER 1

Killing the crow was how the trip began. I should have known that things could only get worse.

The violent death of the bird was telling me NOT to try and climb *Shiva Direct* that day.

I was riding my motorbike at the time. My Tibetan girlfriend Tashi was on the back. We had finished work at the refugee camp and were heading out for a weekend's climbing on one of Nepal's most challenging cliffs.

'It looks like another dust storm is coming in,' Tashi shouted in my ear. 'Sure you don't want to change your mind, Ryan?'

A great reddish-brown cloud was massing ominously on the horizon.

These dry storms had become a regular scourge in this zone of Nepal. The monsoon summer rains had failed for two years in a row. Topsoil was blown off thousands of desiccated fields, countless tons of airborne dust particles merging with ferocious thermal currents.

The result was lightning, not rain.

The local farmers spoke of these storms in superstitious tones. They were generated by evil spirits, they whispered, by devils and demons.

Lightning bolts had struck the camp we worked at on numerous occasions in recent months. Forest fires had raged close by.

I twisted the accelerator. The motorbike engine throbbed like an angry wasp.

Ahead of us I could see the cliffs. A little kick of adrenaline swept through my body.

It was a well-timed trip. A wild experience out here would help me focus on my dilemma. My university back in England had written with a final ultimatum: take up my place to study as a vet, or lose the offer for good.

Trouble was I was still obsessed with climbing Everest. That was why I was hanging out in Nepal, hoping I could find a way back to the mountain.

I saw an obstacle ahead, birds pecking at some sort of

roadkill.

'Ten points for a crow!' I laughed. I accelerated a little, just for a joke.

The first of the birds launched skywards, flapping clear. Others followed. I saw the roadkill was a young deer.

One of the crows was not so sharp.

It hit the visor of my helmet with a sickening thud. Tashi screamed. The air filled with feathers and a thin spray of blood.

I stopped the motorbike. The bird was lying dead behind us. Crumpled. Broken.

'Poor thing,' Tashi shook her head, looking pale.

I took a tissue and tried to scrape my visor clean, succeeding only in spreading the blood across it.

'Bad karma,' Tashi said. A moment later she ran to the verge and was sick.

We kept heading north, the remains of the poor crow gradually congealing in front of my eyes.

I was seeing the world through a haze of blood.

But I was too stupid to see what it meant.

A year had passed since Tashi and I had been on Everest.

We had shared an incredible adventure together on the

North Face.

But we hadn't summited. The ultimate Everest experience was still waiting.

Hardly a day went by that we didn't talk about going back. Hardly a day went by that I didn't take my precious Everest books out of the battered tin trunk that contained my possessions, poring over the images of that most magical of peaks.

Now we were working in a refugee camp in Nepal, helping to care for the thousands of Tibetans who had crossed the border in search of a new life. Tashi was Tibetan as well, forced out of her homeland by the repressive policies of the Chinese government.

Most evenings, after the potato peeling and washing-up had finished, Tashi and I would take a trek to the top of a small hill next to the camp.

From there we could see Everest. Far away in the distance. Enigmatic. Alluring. Inescapable.

I normally took my camera and telephoto lens, capturing the ways the different moods of light played on the high slopes.

'How are you going to get this mountain out of your system?' Tashi asked me one time with a smile. 'Is it even possible?'

'Only one way,' I replied. 'Reach the top.'

She squeezed my arm.

'You need help,' she laughed.

'I'd prefer 50,000 dollars,' I said. 'Buy my way on to a team.'

We walked back to the camp, hand in hand as the final rays of light fell across the Himalaya. Both of us knew my Everest dream was likely to stay just that – a dream.

Life was simple in the camp but these were uncertain times for Nepal. The collapse of the monsoon had cast a dark shadow over the lands around the refugee centre.

Hunger was in the eyes of the children who came to the camp gates looking for scraps. Dust storms whipped through the valleys. Vultures scoured the skies, looking for animals too weak to resist another day without water, without fodder.

A ticking environmental clock was pushing the people of Nepal closer and closer to the edge.

A clock was ticking for me too. A different type of count-down, but one just as pressing.

'I feel like I'm split down the middle,' I confessed to Tashi. 'One version of me wants to go back to England, qualify as a vet, help my parents with the family farm. The other version … well, you know … '

Tashi looked at me with those jet-black Tibetan eyes. She had been so patient with me, far more patient than I deserved.

'You need a sign,' she said.

'A sign?' I laughed. 'Like a bolt from the blue?'

'Could be anything,' Tashi laughed. 'Fate needs to decide for you.'

'Maybe.'

'Why don't we go to the Buddha Cliffs?' Tashi said. 'Climb one of those big routes we've had our eyes on? Maybe a change of scene will help you make up your mind?'

We filled up my motorbike with petrol and packed our climbing gear in a rucksack.

Two hours later, after the crow incident, we reached the Buddha Cliffs.

'Got to love this place,' Tashi said.

The location was spectacular; a vast wall of rock into which a ten-metre-high Buddha figure had been carved. Pilgrims flocked to the spot. Climbers too.

We had no money to pay for a guesthouse; our trip was low budget, wild camping in a leaky old canvas tent. Food was basic that night, a plate of pasta daubed in tomato sauce.

We camped close to the crag, pitching the tent on ground so baked by an unrelenting sun that it felt like sleeping on concrete.

I reached into my pocket for my lucky charm, the palm-sized metal shrine bell I had been given by my Nepali friends Shreeya and Kami.

It was unusually cold to the touch.

I shivered. The crow incident had been a real downer. I felt stupid for shouting that thing about ten points.

A sense of foreboding suddenly hit me.

A cluster of dark thoughts crowded into my mind.

Neither of us had ever been injured on our crazy climbing weekends.

But there was always a first time.

Breakfast was a muesli bar and a cup of sweet tea.

Then we were off to the cliff, ropes draped over our shoulders, harnesses jangling with the metal chinking of karabiners and other bits of climbing gear.

'Let's do a couple of warm-up routes,' Tashi said.

The morning went well and my depression lifted. Half a dozen pitches with Tashi put me in a great mood, the climbing challenging and fun.

A couple of other groups turned up, students from a nearby college and some serious Nepali rock athletes we had seen profiled in climbing magazines.

We had sandwiches for lunch, sheltering beneath a twisted old jacaranda tree. A distant rumble of thunder broke the air and Tashi turned towards me.

'How about the two of us try *Shiva Direct*?'

A jolt of adrenaline rushed through me.

Shiva Direct was a classic, graded at a level I aspired to but had never yet achieved.

Climbing it successfully would be a total rush.

We finished off our cheese butties and trekked up to the cliff face. *Shiva Direct* soared above us, a blunt and uncompromising wall of vertical rock many hundreds of metres high.

'Better get a move on,' Tashi said. She pointed to the south where the brooding front of a new dust storm was now gathered. 'You want to lead?'

I didn't need to be asked twice.

We uncoiled the rope and I tied on. Minutes later I was making moves on the route, climbing rapidly up the strenuous first section, relieved to find a range of decent handholds and footholds.

'Nice work, Ryan,' Tashi called up. 'Looking good.'

There were no bolts on the wall. The climb relied on my own skill at finding protection. Every five or six metres I had to find a natural feature, which I could exploit as an anchor.

A blustering wind began. My body swayed with the power of it. The rock became more challenging as the friendly features of the lower section gave way to a more hostile environment.

Handholds became finger jams. Platforms that could take a whole foot became narrow cracks in which a toehold was the best that could be hoped for.

I found myself losing track of time. The problem-solving aspect of climbing meant my mind was utterly focused and absorbed. All the everyday cares of life simply dissolved on a route like this.

'Get some protection in,' Tashi called up.

I looked down, finding to my surprise that I had ascended almost half a rope length without putting in any safety gear.

I slotted a camming device into a crack and clipped the rope into it with a karabiner.

'Come on up,' I told Tashi. She began to climb, supported by the belay I had rigged.

Another wind front throbbed through the air. A blast of skin-stinging dust hit the crag. A handful of gravel came pinging down the cliff. I pressed my face close to the rock, the little stones clattering off the plastic shell of my helmet.

A warning. The wind was dislodging loose debris. Anything bigger could get serious.

I felt my hair prickle. The dust storm was loading the air with static.

'My brain's beginning to buzz,' Tashi called up. Her voice was clipped, serious. 'We need to get off this route.'

I stared down the cliff, my heart sinking as I saw how high we were. Abseiling down would be complicated and time-consuming.

I craned my neck in the other direction, staring up the cliff. Half a pitch above us was a break in the sheer rock.

'It looks like there's a ledge,' I told her. 'I'll take a look.'

A slender crack split the route above me. I finger-jammed my way up it, my knuckles raw and bloodied by the sharp granite. Lightning flashed on the crag top. The air was humming with electric charge.

The dust was thicker now, a lung-clogging red haze.

The route became overhanging. My feet scrambled for purchase in a crumbling crack. I could feel lactic acid building in the muscles of my arms. My breathing began to accelerate.

The route had a sting in the tail.

I gritted my teeth, hurriedly smashing in a piton, the steel singing with the hammer blows as a further electric roar filled the valley.

A sling gave me protection. Three stretchy moves got me through the hard section. I got to the ledge and jugged up on to it.

A quick glance told me what I needed to know. The ledge was a perfect refuge from the wind and lightning, a stony platform with a scooped-out little overhang at the back.

'There's space for both of us,' I yelled.

Just to the left of the cave was a convenient spike of rock. I draped a sling over it and snapped the rope on with a figure-of eight device.

'Climb when you're ready,' I called down. A muffled cry from Tashi came back and I tightened up the line as the anchor took her weight.

Five minutes later I could hear her panting on the crux section below me. The sound of her boots jamming into the tiny footholds. An occasional grunt. Then two ripped-up hands clutched at the rock ledge and a dust-covered face popped up.

'Nice find!' Tashi exclaimed. She flopped on to the rocky platform beside me.

Two minutes of co-ordinated shuffling got us side by side, pressed into the tiny cave. I shivered as the wind rocked us again.

A flash of intense light ripped the air. Ear-splitting thunder a second later.

'Dust storm getting closer,' Tashi muttered.

The sharp, explosive smell of scorched rock swept down. There was a sulphurous tang to the air. A boulder tumbled heavily down the cliff face, passing just a few metres to the left of our ledge.

'You still call this fun?' Tashi smiled.

'Let's have a brew.'

I shrugged off the little backpack, opening it up carefully and taking out the few items it contained. An emergency foil blanket. My drinks flask. A compact camera. A balaclava and spare set of gloves.

A glint of metal caught Tashi's eye.

'Should have known you'd have your talisman along for the ride,' she said.

She picked up the object, the brass bell that I kept close to me at all times.

'You know how it is,' I told her. 'Superstition and all that.'

Tashi turned the little bell in her hands, tracing the engravings one by one.

'I remember how you carried this on Everest,' she said. 'Maybe it really did bring us luck.'

Tashi held the polished wooden handle and shook the bell, the delicate 'ting' sounding alien and bizarrely out of place amidst the elemental roar of the storm.

'We might need a prayer or two,' she remarked. 'Help us get off this climb in one piece.'

She frowned, juggling the bell from one hand to the other.

'Strange,' she passed it back to me. 'It feels like it's alive.'

I cradled the bell in my hands, my fingers tingling as the object throbbed. The metal bell was acting as a conductor, the atmosphere alive with lightning charge.

I had experienced similar events in other electrical storms. Ice axes could spit out sparks as tens of thousands of volts raged through the air.

We could hear it buzzing in our ears. I could taste it, ferrous, on my tongue.

'Whoa!' The bell began to heat up. Suddenly it was red hot.

My fingers fumbled. I dropped it. The bell tumbled on to the ledge, bouncing instantly towards the drop.

Tashi gasped.

I lunged out, snatching the bell as it bounced.

At that precise moment a deafening explosion rent

the air. A blinding flash came with it. For the briefest of moments I felt I had been speared through the shoulder. I saw Tashi's eyes wide with shock.

I smelled burning flesh.

Then everything went dark.

Crazy dreams assailed me. My mind had lost track of where or who I was. I felt myself shivering with cold, my voltage-jarred brain concluding I was buried in snow.

An avalanche had swept me away? Was that what had happened?

Like my friend Kami, I was trapped underneath tons of snow and ice. My body was damaged. I could sense pain but it seemed to be everywhere. I moved my arm, thinking to dig myself out.

Then I saw Kami's face. My Nepali friend. He was talking to me from the bed that was now his permanent world, a paralysed prison in which he would spend the rest of his life.

'You're going to make it, Ryan,' he was whispering. 'Don't give up.'

I came to with a jolt, super groggy, still utterly unsure as to what was going on.

Tashi's face was just inches from mine.

Wind continued to whip around us. Had I fallen? Was I concussed?

'The local guys saw what happened. They're coming up,' Tashi said, her voice cracking up with emotion. 'They're going to rope you off, Ryan, do you understand?'

I nodded.

All I had to do was wait, concentrating on Tashi's face; grey, creased with concern, her eyes two dark pools of fear. She spoke often but her words were lost, my ears were humming with a high-pitched distortion that sounded as loud as a pneumatic drill.

'Hang in there, Ryan,' was all I heard. Then her words faded like the daylight.

I drifted in and out of consciousness as the Nepali climbers arrived at our little ledge, shifting me on to a mountain stretcher and lowering me into the void.

The college minibus became a makeshift ambulance. I rolled around on the back seat as it bucked up the potholed track for what seemed like a thousand miles.

Back at the refugee camp a nurse cut the sleeve off my Gore-Tex jacket. I sucked my breath in sharply as I saw my scorched flesh.

'You're lucky,' the doctor said. 'Not many people survive

a lightning strike.'

Lightning. Of course. My brain snapped back into something close to a functioning mode. I had reached for the shrine bell. The bolt had hit home. Right in the shoulder.

'OK Ryan,' the doctor continued. 'Let's take a look.'

The gentle crackle of burning firewood coaxed my hearing back to life.

My eyes focused. Pain swam into view.

Tashi was there, holding my hand.

'Welcome back,' she said gently. 'You've been unconscious for two days.'

I began to learn about my injury.

The lightning had scored a direct hit on the top of my right arm, searing a sickle-shaped burn right around the top of my shoulder and up to the base of my neck.

It hurt like mad. But I was lucky to be alive.

In the split second after the lightning strike I had fallen forward, out of control. Unroped at that moment, I would have been killed by a fall down the entire face if Tashi hadn't grabbed my harness.

The shape of the wound, which they likened to a crescent moon, fascinated the superstitious Tibetans at the camp.

Slipping off my shirt for crowd inspections became a daily ritual as the refugees discussed in laborious detail the various possible messages that fate had been trying to send me.

'They cannot decide if it was a good omen or a bad one,' Tashi said.

'Seriously?' I laughed. 'Getting struck by lightning and almost falling off a cliff is "lucky" by Tibetan standards?'

'It could be,' Tashi said. 'It might influence your life in an important way.'

More of the refugees arrived, chatting excitedly about the chance to inspect the English patient. A man with a smartphone began taking pictures of my injury.

'I should sell tickets,' I told Tashi. 'I'd make a fortune.'

My rucksack had also been hit. Half of it was now an incinerated blob. Tashi did her best to salvage a climbing sling and a jacket from it, but they were welded to the melted nylon of the pack and completely beyond help.

'What's this?'

She plucked a charred sheet of paper from the pack.

It was the university form. I had taken it with me, thinking I'd fill it in and return it after the trip.

Tashi handed me the burned crisp of paper.

'Wow.' I was speechless for a few moments. The form was utterly destroyed.

'You wanted a sign,' she said. 'You certainly got one.'

'What date is it today?' I asked.

We calculated that there were still a few hours to get the form re-sent from the UK, to fill it in and commit myself to university.

But the lightning strike had helped me make up my mind. And once I had made the decision, it felt like the right one.

It wasn't just about uni or no uni.

It was about Everest. And the unfinished business that still haunted me.

Reaching the ultimate summit was still my dream. Somehow I had to find a way to do it.

Normal life could wait.

Gradually my injury stabilised. Pain relief helped me to sleep. My wound was cleaned and sterilised and redressed every day. The camp's directors offered to get me into one of the big hospitals in Kathmandu, but I didn't want to be so far away from Tashi so I elected to stay in my tent.

A hospital room might have been more hygienic but I had become used to the slight squalor of the camp and reckoned I would survive.

A week went by. My body was adjusting to the damage. Then Tashi came to my tent in a state of great excitement.

'You'll never guess what I just heard,' Tashi said. Her pretty face, usually wreathed with smiles, was even more radiant than usual.

'What?'

'The Dalai Lama is coming to visit the camp!'

'No way!'

'Yes! He's on an official visit to Nepal. When he found out how many Tibetan refugees are here, he put us on the itinerary.'

'Kharma will be gutted when he finds out what he's missing,' I exclaimed. Tashi nodded, smiling at the thought of her mischievous brother. Unable to find any work in Nepal, he had left a couple of months earlier for the Middle East, enticed by tales of high wages on the building sites.

He would be kicking himself when he found out who was visiting the camp. He had kept a portrait of the spiritual leader of the Tibetan people with him ever since he was a child, even though it had led to persecution and punishment by the Chinese.

The camp had to be spotless for the Dalai Lama's visit. A frenzy of painting and cleaning kicked off.

I was confined to my sickbed, cursing my bad luck.

The great day arrived. I had hoped I would be well enough to join in the celebrations, but I was still bed-bound in my tent, my shoulder and arm bandaged tight.

The buzz was intense. This was no normal sleepy morning in Camp Delta. From dawn onwards the excited clamour of conversation filled the air, children's footsteps pounding up and down the path that ran by my tent. I tried not to feel sorry for myself but had to admit I was gutted to be missing out. I was sure I would never get another opportunity to meet the great man.

Suddenly a cry went up.

'The helicopter is coming!'

Tashi burst into the tent, smiling broadly, her cheeks flushed with excitement. She had bought a new dress from the markets in Kathmandu and was wearing it for the first time.

'What do you think?' She flashed me a cheeky grin, performing a pirouette in the middle of the tent, rays of sunlight punching through the holes in the canvas roof, picking out the rainbow colours of her dress.

'Gorgeous,' I managed to croak. It was the first time I had seen Tashi wearing anything but trekking clothes and

I found myself slightly lost for words.

'They got a radio call,' she said. 'He's going to be here in five minutes!'

Tashi poured me some tea from a flask and produced a couple of sugared dosas – local pancakes – from a wrap of paper.

'I'll take some photos for you,' she said. She kissed me and rushed out of the tent as the helicopter swooped overhead.

I finished my lonely breakfast and listened to the cheers and chanting and singing that greeted the Dalai Lama. The outpouring of affection was hardly surprising given the great man's status as a living god to the people of Tibet.

Most of the refugees in the camp had spent their lives under Chinese rule, forbidden to talk about the Dalai Lama or even own a photograph of him. Now, exiled in the free country of Nepal, away from the oppressive all-seeing eye of Chinese spies, they were free to express their true feelings.

It was a celebration, Tibetan style, the air alive with the crackle of fireworks, the clash of cymbals and the bass drone of huge brass trumpets.

I tried to concentrate on my book but just couldn't focus.

Gradually I heard the procession getting closer to my tent. The honoured visitor was getting a tour of the camp.

Seconds later the tent flap was pulled to one side and Tashi dashed in.

'What's happening?' I blurted.

She snatched armfuls of clothes from the floor, stuffing them behind my bed.

'He's coming in!' she hissed.

'What?' I looked around the tent in horror. The place was a total tip and I hadn't had a shave or a shower for days so I looked – and no doubt smelled – pretty much like a tramp.

Too late. Three heartbeats later the tent flaps opened again. A saffron-robed figure stepped inside.

CHAPTER 2

'Is this the English boy you told me about?' the Dalai Lama asked Tashi.

'Yes, Your Holiness.'

I raised myself up, leaning on my good arm.

'Please,' my visitor smiled as he pulled up a chair. 'Don't move too much on my account. From what I've heard of your adventures, it might be better you rest.'

'S ... s ... s ... sorry about the mess,' I stammered. A visit from one of the holiest men on the planet was the last thing I was expecting.

He shrugged, as if it was of no concern. His whole manner was very matter of fact and open; he was a natural communicator without a shred of ego or grand pretensions.

'The people of the camp are speaking about you,' His Holiness said with a smile. 'They seem to think your survival was some sort of miracle!'

'It was my friend here that saved me,' I replied. Tashi smiled modestly as the Dalai Lama turned, nodding kindly to her.

'You are a man of the mountains, I hear,' my visitor chuckled. 'So lightning strike is an occupational hazard, one might say.'

'Maybe,' I laughed. 'But I'm not going to make a habit of it.'

'How long will you take to heal?'

'It's too early to say, sir,' I replied. 'But I hope I'll be back in the mountains soon.'

'Rest is the thing,' he said. 'Stay here until you regain your strength. I'm sure they are looking after you well.'

'Your Holiness … ?' An official coughed politely.

The Dalai Lama's entourage was clearly keen to resume the tour of the camp.

The great man patted my undamaged hand.

'I wish you a rapid recovery,' he said.

He rose to his feet then suddenly froze, his attention caught by something on the trunk next to my camp bed.

'A shrine bell,' he exclaimed. 'May I take a look?'

24

He picked up the bell, cradling it in his hands, examining it closely. His eyebrows rose. An expression of surprise creased his noble face. He looked inside, scratching gently at the interior surface of the metal with his fingernail.

The other monks could not contain their curiosity. They leaned in also, watching the actions of their spiritual leader intently.

'Sometimes the monasteries put a mark inside,' the Dalai Lama said. 'There's a lot of dirt and dust collected but let me see … '

He scraped for a few moments then asked me, 'Have you got a torch?'

Tashi found a head torch next to the bed.

'There's a seal stamped into the metal,' he said.

He let out a gentle 'hmmm' of surprise.

'What is it?' Tashi and the others gathered in even closer.

'How old do you think this bell is?' the Dalai Lama asked.

'I don't know,' I replied. 'Maybe fifty or sixty years?'

He shook his head. 'Look at this mark in the metal.'

He handed me the shrine bell and the torch. Tashi came over to me and we looked inside, seeing a faint seal stamped into the brass.

'I've only seen one shrine bell like this before,' the Dalai Lama said slowly. 'And that was at the Barkhor temple.'

'Really?' Tashi looked impressed.

'I think this may be hundreds of years old and I believe it might have belonged to someone rather special.'

'Like who, sir?' I asked.

'That mark is the seal of the seventh Dalai Lama.'

The other monks stared at each other when they heard these words. Tashi drew in her breath.

'There's powerful magic in this object,' the Dalai Lama said. 'I felt it the first moment I saw it.'

'My friends Kami and Shreeya certainly thought so,' I said. 'They believe it will go to the summit of Everest one day.'

For a moment I thought that the great man was going to speak further. Then he smiled.

'We will see,' he said simply.

A photographer entered the tent.

'Just a quick shot please,' he said.

He took a photograph of me and the Dalai Lama, the shrine bell still cradled in his hands.

Then the great man and his entourage left.

A hot month went by. My shoulder slowly healed.

Tashi's family gave me local remedies, herbs and extracts of plants, which were applied in a paste directly on to my skin.

The refugee camp doctor was amazed at the effectiveness of these traditional medicines.

'I thought you would need a skin graft,' she said. 'But the wound has healed better than I thought.'

Tashi smiled. She had always had complete faith in the power of natural cures.

While I recovered, the security situation in Nepal gradually worsened.

We had seen the country deteriorating as the drought had gripped. The failure of the second rice harvest had been a depressing blow for the people of Nepal, and led to a sharp spike in crime.

Village stores had been robbed.

The police had been selling sacks of grain, which were supposed to be distributed free.

The government had not allocated a single dollar of the billions of aid dollars donated by ordinary people all over the world.

Then came a special day.

'Happy birthday, Ryan.' Tashi brought my favourite milky coffee to the tent then gave me a long hug.

My parents called from England. Distant voices from a world that no longer felt like my own. A couple of the refugee families gave me gifts. Then the camp's commander broke the spell by handing me a shovel and getting me to dig a ditch down in the lower part of the camp.

It was a backbreaker of a job and a good test for my injured shoulder. The tendons complained but I managed to do the task with the help of a couple of painkillers. It was infuriating work though; for every shovelful of mud I managed to get out of that trench, twice the amount would slide back into the hole.

I worked for a few hours then returned to the canteen to get a late breakfast. Tashi came up behind me. Her hands reaching round to gently cover my eyes.

'I've got a surprise for you,' she said.

'Yeah?'

Tashi always loved pulling tricks on me. It was part of her mischievous character.

I looked around. Everyone was looking at me. I smiled and shrugged, unable to see what had changed.

Then the flap of the tent was pulled aside and two people walked in: a middle-aged Western man, tanned and fit, with a mane of golden hair. And a pretty local girl wearing a traditional silk dress.

I blinked. For a heartbeat I wondered if I was seeing things. *Alex Brennan and Shreeya?*

Two friends from the past, from the very first journey

I made in Nepal.

Two friends I had never expected to see again.

Two friends who had changed my life by introducing me to Everest.

The shock was total. I just stood there like an idiot, figuring that this could NOT be real.

'There's someone who wants to see you,' Alex said.

The tent flap pulled back once more.

'No way,' I whispered.

Tashi gripped my hand.

A third person walked in.

It was *Kami*.

Kami! Walking! For a moment I thought I must be dreaming.

This was the Nepali friend I had last seen lying on his back in a remote clinic far out in the wild mountain ranges. The friend who had been paralysed in an avalanche. The friend who had once climbed to within a stone's throw of the summit of Everest, only to have his dream snatched away from him at the final moment.

Kami who could hardly move, let alone walk.

'Hello Ryan!' he said.

The room went silent.

'You're walking!' I whispered.

He took a few more steps.

'You're *walking*!'

Kami's smile was wide enough to light up even this cloudiest of days. He radiated happiness with so much intensity it touched every single person in that tent.

'Kami!' I ran forward and embraced him.

He was real enough. And so were his tears.

'How did you find me?' I asked.

'Because you're famous,' Shreeya said.

She brought out a crumpled page from a newspaper. The photograph of the Dalai Lama and me was there alongside an article about the holy man's visit to the camp.

'I saw it by chance,' Shreeya said. 'Otherwise we never would have tracked you down.'

A regular old hug-in followed. I introduced Tashi to everyone and Alex explained to her that he had been the expedition leader on Kami's fateful Everest climb, later giving up his ambitions to be a politician in the USA and building a remote clinic to care for his paralysed Nepali friend.

We sat at the table, joining the others for a cup of tea. I kept staring at my friends, just so happy to see them.

'How did this happen?' I asked. 'What magic spell did you use to get Kami walking again?'

'It *was* magic,' Shreeya said.

'Stem cell magic,' Alex added.

We ate rice and lentils, catching up on two years of news.

'Even though I was something of a recluse out there at the clinic, I was still in contact with a few old buddies from my Harvard days,' Alex said. 'One of them is a leading expert in stem-cell technology and it turned out he was working on a new treatment.'

'He's a miracle worker,' Shreeya said.

'I was a guinea pig,' Kami added proudly, savouring his use of the words.

'I told this buddy about Kami's injury,' Alex continued. 'And he came out to Nepal to check things out. We helicoptered Kami out to Kathmandu so my friend could do some scans. He was honest about the risks but reckoned it was worth a try.'

'Alex got us passports and visas for the USA,' Shreeya said. 'We flew to Washington on a special flight so that Kami's stretcher could be loaded on.'

'It was always my dream to go to America,' Kami said. 'But I have to say it was strange to arrive flat on my back. I couldn't even see any of the views out of the ambulance window as they drove me to the hospital.'

'They took OECs from Kami's nasal cavity,' Alex continued. 'That's olfactory ensheathing cells – the type of stem cells that have the power to reconnect tissue. They cultured them in the lab until they had several million.'

'That was the easy bit,' Kami smiled.

'Then they removed four strips of nerve tissue from his ankle,' Alex went on. 'And inserted it into the spinal cord where the damage was.'

'They did about 200 injections into my neck,' Kami said, shuddering with the memory. 'They called them micro-injections but they didn't feel so micro to me.'

Alex took over. 'The stem cells encourage the nerve tissue to connect. Build a new bridge between the two severed ends of Kami's spinal cord.'

'After three months I could feel my legs,' Kami said. 'After six I was taking the first steps. I was walking within a year.'

'Check out the video,' Alex said.

He brought out a laptop and fired it up. Seconds later we were looking at images of Kami's fight to walk.

The pictures showed Kami, strapped into a hoist in a rehab centre. Shreeya and several medical staff were in the room. The hoist came down, allowing him to place his legs on the floor. Kami was standing upright, a huge smile on his face.

'That was the first stage,' Kami said. 'All the muscles in my legs had atrophied. I needed to regain some strength;

get used to supporting my own weight again.'

'The physio has been brutal,' Alex said, sipping his tea. 'Five hours a day, almost every day since the operation. It's truly down to Kami's determination that he's made so much progress.'

The images changed. Now we saw Kami helped on to a treadmill. Alex Brennan was there, looking on proudly.

Slowly, with an expression of utmost concentration, Kami took a tentative step on the treadmill. The spectators broke into a spontaneous round of applause. Shreeya embraced him with tears in her eyes.

'That was the first step since the accident,' Kami said.

'From there, things moved really quickly,' Shreeya told us. 'He could walk almost normally by six months, and we were married a few weeks later. After one year, well, you see how he is.'

'I want to go to Base Camp,' Kami said. 'Get close to Everest again.'

And that reminded me. About the shrine bell.

I rushed to my tent and found it. Returning to the canteen, I placed the shrine bell in Kami's hands.

'This,' Kami said, turning the bell in his hands, 'is a moment I have been waiting for, for a very long time.'

Tashi told the story of our Everest North Face adventure,

how the shrine bell had been with us on our clandestine climb, how we had rescued her wounded brother Kharma from above 8,000 metres.

'I want to see the route,' Kami insisted.

We found a book containing a photo of the North Face, talking Kami and Alex through our climb with a blow-by-blow account.

'So that's twice the shrine bell has been high on Everest,' Kami said. 'Surely the third time it will reach the top?'

'The Dalai Lama was fascinated by it,' Tashi said. 'He revealed its true origins.'

We told the story of the great man's visit. His revelation about the age and sanctity of the shrine bell.

Kami searched inside the metal bell, showed the inscription proudly to Shreeya, whose family had been the original owners before she had gifted it to him.

'Your family never told you about this?' he asked.

Shreeya shook her head.

'I knew it had been handed down from father to son for many generations,' she said. 'But no one ever told me it was so ancient.'

She looked proud enough to burst.

'In that case, we must honour it even more,' Kami said.

Later that day, one of the workers at the camp took us all to a nearby valley to see his brother's farm. We walked down a dirt track for a mile, following the dry ruin of an irrigation ditch.

The farm was carved out of rocky terrain. The fields were barren. The earth cracked and split, desiccated by drought. A few straggly shoots poked from the mud but they were already withered.

The farmer and his young wife welcomed us with dignity, but, following the traditional greetings, the farmer's first words revealed his state of mind.

'Have you any news of the monsoon?' he asked urgently. 'Will it fail for a third time?'

Somehow our hosts had got the wrong idea, thinking we were meteorological experts. In fact we had no news to offer. The workings of the great Asian weather system were as much a mystery to us as they were to the people of Nepal.

He showed us a dried-up ditch.

'This is the canal our farm depends on,' he said. 'It's been totally dry for two years.'

'How about groundwater?' Alex asked.

The farmer's wife took us to the family well, drawing

a bucket of brackish, muddy water.

'Things would be better if we had a water pump,' the farmer said. 'But equipment like that is beyond our reach …'

All of us knew that water pumps cost a fortune in Nepal. Then there was the drilling operation, the borehole that would tap fresh water deep beneath the earth.

Finally would be the cost of the fuel to power the pump.

Most of the local farmers were already up to their necks in debt. More credit was the last thing they needed to take on, especially with loan sharks roaming the countryside, lending money at punitive interest rates and seizing land ruthlessly when monthly payments were late.

The farmer showed us his food store. It contained just half a sack of mouldy rice.

'We've never known the monsoon fail before,' he said. 'The summer rains are our very lifeblood.'

'It always arrived in the first or second week of June,' his wife lamented. 'Every year of our lives. What is happening to the weather? Is it true that the whole world is heating up? Is that why the monsoon has failed?'

We had no answers, but it seemed climate change was to blame.

The farmer invited us into his house. We were served

tea and offered biscuits which we knew must have been purchased especially for our visit – probably with money the family could ill afford to spend.

Generosity of spirit was such a genuine part of the Nepali character.

His two children were thin as rakes, with the telltale distended bellies of malnutrition. They stared at the biscuits with wide, hungry eyes.

'We've had no crop to sell for two years,' the farmer told us. 'The children have had to leave school because we don't have money. If the monsoon fails again, I don't know what we will do. Maybe I will have to abandon the farm and take the family to Kathmandu.'

We gave the children our biscuits and Tashi took them out to play.

Alex had been quiet up until this point. Now he spoke up.

'I will pay for your children to go to school,' he said. 'And buy you the water pump you need.'

The farmer nodded, too overwhelmed to reply. His wife suggested we pray at the family shrine and Kami got his first opportunity to ring the shrine bell.

We returned to the refugee camp, saddened by what we had seen.

'We've helped one family,' Alex said. 'But look at this land, at the thousands of families facing the same situation.'

He gestured at the withered terraces, at the dust blowing from the degraded soil. The water pumps, silent because no farmer could afford the fuel. The children gathered listlessly by the roadsides, too tired to play.

Back at the refugee camp Tashi and I went to work in the kitchens. It felt downright wrong to be peeling mounds of potatoes after visiting the farm – to be in the presence of so much food. In some ways the Tibetan refugees we cared for were actually better off than the Nepali family we had just met.

They had three meals a day. Food flown in on aeroplanes from the USA. Medical care. A school for the children.

But the Tibetans we cared for had a different set of problems. They were in exile from their homeland. Often, they were apart from their closest family members, dreaming only of the day they could return to a free Tibet.

'You know, the truth is sad,' Tashi said. 'No one here is living the life they want. No one.'

Kami had been quiet since our visit to the farm. The farmer's plight had really affected him. After supper I suggested we take a stroll to the top of the hill that overlooked the camp, the place where Everest could be seen in the distance.

I thought it might cheer him up.

We trekked up the trail, side by side, Kami a little slow but doing well. It was the first time we had walked anywhere together – the Kami I had known before had been confined to his bed.

The air was filled with the fragrant aroma of burning juniper. Many of the camp's residents burned it to make special devotions. A nightingale was singing somewhere in the forest below the camp, an ever-varied song of great beauty which gave the evening a special charm.

A pack of rhesus macaque monkeys followed us up the trail, chattering and squabbling. They were the scavengers of the camp, hoping to be thrown a scrap of food. The failure of the monsoon had been bad for them as well.

At the top of the rise was a small meadow. From there we could see Everest, far on the horizon. The air was hazy with grey-blue smoke, so the mountain appeared veiled behind the mist.

'More mysterious than ever,' Kami said. 'It still works a type of magic on me.'

'Me too,' I told him. 'I can't escape it.'

Kami brought out the shrine bell, turning it over and over in his hands.

'There is a final chapter to be told,' he said. 'The Dalai

Lama has predicted it.'

'A third time on Everest for the shrine bell?' I smiled. 'It's not impossible.'

Kami's face suddenly lit up. He caught my arm.

'How about we take it to Base Camp?' Kami said suddenly. 'We can build a cairn – hold a puja ceremony. Pray for the monsoon to come back this year. Pray for the people to have food.'

I had to smile at Kami's incredible level of faith. He truly believed that his idea could change things, that a single prayer at Base Camp could unlock a type of magic that would change the fate of millions.

It summed up his personality so well. His purity of spirit. His inner fire.

'Do you reckon you could do the trek?' I asked. 'Is your body up to it?'

'There's only one way to find out,' he said. 'I think I can do it, and my body will just have to keep up with my mind!'

'You're stubborn enough!' I laughed.

'I'm going to talk to Alex about it,' he said.

Back in the tent, Kami's proposal created much excitement.

'It's a wonderful idea,' Shreeya said. 'The perfect way to celebrate your new lease of life!'

'The gods will be on your side,' Tashi beamed. 'They will

look down and protect you every inch of the way.'

Alex sipped on his tea for a few moments then sighed theatrically.

'I had a feeling something like this might happen,' he said.

He turned to Tashi and me.

'Want to come?'

Of course we said yes. The chance to get close to Everest again was too good to miss.

For Tashi, it was a chance to explore Nepal in more depth. So far she had seen little more than the refugee camp and the valleys immediately around it. Her parents were a bit nervous about the lawlessness that had spread through the country but they supported her decision to go.

Nevertheless, it felt a bit wrong to be bailing out on the refugee camp when things were so busy. Tibetans were still crossing into Nepal on a daily basis, on the run from Chinese oppression.

'We have worked solidly without a break for a whole year,' Tashi reminded me. 'Three weeks off is fair enough, don't you think?'

The camp's director was sympathetic. And there were

other volunteers who could take our place. We opened up the storage trunk in the tent and pulled out our trekking gear and wet-weather clothes with all the excitement of children unwrapping presents on Christmas Day.

'I was thinking about something,' Tashi told me. 'About the sequence of events that led to all this happening.'

'How do you mean?'

'The lightning strike was where it all began. And if it hadn't been for that, the Dalai Lama would never have visited you in the tent and seen the shrine bell. Then the photograph was taken and Shreeya happened to see it. They would never have found you if it weren't for that series of events.'

'A chain reaction,' I said. 'You're right.'

It was an extraordinary thought. The lightning strike had set things in motion.

We agreed to leave the next morning. Kami and the others were put up at the camp for the night.

Back in my tent, I packed my rucksack and climbed into bed.

It felt strange to be without the shrine bell. The tent seemed empty without it. The bell had been so close to me, my most treasured belonging. I had come to think of it almost as a part of myself.

But it had never really been mine. Kami and Shreeya

had given it to me to see if I could get it to the summit of Mount Everest.

And I had not completed that quest.

Kami had always been the true owner.

Now it was about to take its third journey to the mountain.

CHAPTER 3

Our journey by jeep to Kathmandu revealed just how bad things were getting in the countryside. It was nine months since the second rice harvest had failed and hunger was beginning to bite. Nepali families were walking along the highways carrying huge bags of possessions.

'Where are they going?' Shreeya asked.

'Anywhere they can find food,' Kami replied.

Kathmandu was heaving with refugees, the streets humming with people on the move. Makeshift shelters had been erected on every available scrap of ground. The military parade ground in the centre of town was packed with tents and tarpaulins. People were even living in the middle of roundabouts.

I saw some Red Cross food stations giving out cooked rice. The queues at those were every bit as long as the ones for petrol.

'People come here to try and find jobs,' Kami said. 'But the city is already full. There are no jobs left.'

Kathmandu airport was tense. There were more troops around than normal and even a tank stationed at the entrance.

'Things are getting stressful,' Alex observed. 'Nepal is heading to a dark place.'

The soldiers stopped us. Our tickets were examined carefully and our passports checked out.

When we finally got into the terminal we discovered our flight to the mountain airstrip of Lukla was delayed.

'A fuel delivery is on the way,' the operations manager told us.

Bad-tempered mountaineers were pacing the airport terminal, waiting for their Everest dream to start.

Some had planned their climb for years.

Seven hours went by in the mosquito-infested departures lounge. Not a single flight went out. A one-legged man with a tea trolley and an urn did good business on his hourly tour, pouring sweet black tea by the gallon.

Alex was recognised by a couple of American tourists; his high-profile days as a senator still remembered by some.

Just when we were thinking of abandoning our hopes of flying into the mountains, activity began. A fuel tanker was spotted out on the tarmac. I saw the plane pulled out of a hangar, a twenty-seat, propeller-driven veteran, which looked like it was one flight away from the great aircraft graveyard in the sky.

It was Shreeya's first flight. She clutched Kami's hand tight as we walked to the aircraft.

'One of the tyres is flat,' Kami said with a twinkle in his eye.

Shreeya was praying as the plane taxied out to the runway and she shrieked as we rose into the sky.

'I'm getting a strange sense of déjà vu,' Alex said as we gained height and swung towards the mountains. He had been withdrawn in the airport departures lounge, and I sensed he had mixed feelings about the trip.

It was hardly surprising. Alex's previous Everest expedition with Kami had changed both of their lives in so many ways.

'I really thought I would never go back,' he said.

Our destination was Lukla, the fabled gateway to the Himalaya. Landing on the tiny runway has been a rite of passage for Everest travellers ever since Sir Edmund Hillary carved it out of the hillside in the 1960s.

We bumped down forty minutes later, climbing out into the super-chilled air of the mountain town.

Even here the signs of stress were all too evident. We were told a riot had kicked off only the day before, with hundreds of youths fighting against police.

There were scores of military men around and the mood was still tense.

As we collected our baggage from the back of the plane, a huge helicopter came in to land. A great plume of dust kicked up, making us cough and filling our eyes with grit. I saw half a dozen climbers jump out of the aircraft, followed by a young girl dressed in trekking gear. She smiled as she looked out across the mountains; her blonde bunches highlighted by the sun.

'I know that girl,' Alex said. 'I met her father during my days in politics. She's Anatoly Kuzkin's daughter.'

'Kuzkin?' Tashi said. 'The oil guy?'

I was also familiar with Kuzkin's name. The oligarch was rumoured to be the one of the wealthiest men in the world, certainly the richest in Russia. Oil exploration had made him his first fortune and mining for undersea metals was making him another.

'She's a lovely kid,' Alex said. 'Despite her father being a monster.'

A large crowd of porters was pushing at the airport gate, causing us to be momentarily trapped inside the arrivals hall. The helicopter passengers were alongside us and Tashi took the opportunity to say hi to the young Russian.

'Are you trekking up to Everest?' she asked.

'I wish,' the young girl said with a friendly grin. 'Actually we're here to look for a man called Dawa. He's somewhere in this town, we think.'

She gestured to her companion, a sweet-looking Asian woman, who was chatting with some of the airport officials. 'That's Anisa. Dawa is her boyfriend,' she whispered.

Tashi held out her hand.

'I'm Tashi. This is Ryan.'

'My name is Zhanna,' she said. She shook hands with us, her poise quite remarkable for such a young person.

'How old are you?' asked Tashi.

'Twelve,' she replied.

A policeman approached.

'You can leave now,' he said. The porters had been pushed back.

'Maybe see you around town,' Zhanna said.

'Sure.'

She gave us a dazzling smile and left the airport building with a massive gang of porters following on.

'What do you make of her?' Tashi asked.

I laughed. 'A total princess.'

We headed for the centre of Lukla and the accommodation that Alex had arranged. The manager of the lodge met us in the street, rubbing his hands happily, visibly delighted to have a group booked in. He showed us to our rooms, apologising in advance that there was no gas to provide hot showers.

'Supplies have been disrupted,' he said. 'The riots have messed up everything.'

Tashi and I went for a walk before lunch. We quickly got the measure of the place, the slightly squalid Main Street – a glorified alley, in fact – that ran the length of the town.

The atmosphere was a bit strange with so many soldiers around, but shopkeepers still tried to entice us into their stores:

'Map of Base Camp, sir?'

'You need sun hat, madam? I have very cheap sun hat!'

We found a shop selling fake mountain gear, direct copies of famous brands at a fraction of the normal price.

A handful of Polish mountaineers were browsing the racks.

'Without Everest climbers we would be finished,' the storeowner said. 'They come after avalanche. They come after earthquake, during the civil war. Even now in the middle of the famine.'

Everest was ever enduring, it seemed, and powerful enough to attract climbers even in times of turbulence.

'No point giving you the menu,' the lodge manager told us when we gathered for lunch. 'Three quarters of the items are not available.'

'No pizza? No burger? No milkshake?' Kami laughed. 'How are we supposed to trek to Base Camp without them?'

'There's curry and potatoes,' he said. 'And that's it.'

It was actually delicious.

That night we googled Zhanna's father on the iPad.

Most of the links were predictable, profiles in business magazines and brief mentions in the gossip pages of British newspapers.

One of the links caught my eye:

'Russian oligarch denies Indian Ocean damage.'

Anatoly Kuzkin's mining operation in the Indian Ocean is causing an environmental disaster of an unimaginable scale. Ripping millions of tons of metal from the sea floor may be changing the chemistry of the entire Indian Ocean.'

'That must be illegal?' Kami asked.

'International waters,' Alex said. 'He can do what he wants.'

I read on: *'The indiscriminate plundering of the seabed is bad enough, but the effects of Mr Kuzkin's operation do not stop there. Nickel released into the water is causing a vast plume of Methanosarcina microbes to flourish right across the northern Indian Ocean. This organism, a prolific producer of the greenhouse gas methane, is widely believed to have caused the Permian-Triassic extinction event 250 million years ago when ninety-six per cent of all marine species and up to seventy per cent of all land species were wiped out.'*

'Profit,' Tashi commented bitterly. 'All he cares about is making money.'

A map accompanied the piece, showing the extent of Kuzkin's mining exploits in the Indian Ocean. The scale of it was truly staggering, stretching from Kenya right across to India. The Russian had a massive fleet of specialised dredgers out there, working round the clock to rake metal nodules off the sea floor.

The article finished with a plea to sign a petition urging the authorities to put a stop to Kuzkin's enterprise.

Stray dogs were snarling and fighting outside our window that night. Sleep eluded me, partly because of the effects of the altitude, partly from raw excitement for the trek.

'You know what?' Tashi stretched out on the bed and yawned deeply.

'Tell me,' I said, cuddling up to her.

'The higher the altitude, the happier I become,' she said. She was asleep in seconds.

I stayed awake for a while, thinking about Kuzkin. It seemed incredible that one man could cause so much damage.

I wondered if his daughter knew the truth.

The trek began just after dawn. Our little team gathered at the end of the town, expecting to complete the passport checks and paperwork that would allow us into the Everest national park.

'The office is closed,' a passing yak herder told us. 'The workers haven't been paid for six months so they've gone home to their villages.'

It was the same story everywhere. The gradual collapse of government systems.

'Let's go anyway,' Alex said.

We walked through the concrete arch that marked the start of the Everest national park. The air was crisp, a hint of frost sensed with every breath.

I felt a real spring to my step; it was great to be following in the footsteps of the famous 1953 expedition that had put Edmund Hillary and Tenzing Norgay on the summit. My previous climb with Tashi had been on the other side of the mountain, the Tibetan approach from the north.

So all of this was new.

The trekking was exhilarating but hard. The first part of the trail to Base Camp goes against the lay of the land, crossing valley after valley by way of steep cols. Hours of lung-busting effort are required to climb up the dusty tracks to the high points, followed by high-speed, knee-crunching descents back to the valley floor.

Shreeya was not enjoying that first trek. Tashi and I saw her run for the bushes to be sick.

'You OK?' Tashi asked.

'Just adapting,' she said, her face horribly pale.

I was also adapting. To the lightning scars on my shoulder. The rucksack straps bit hard into the tender new tissue, causing me to grit my teeth.

'Put on more padding,' Tashi urged, inspecting the damage. We strapped on more bandages, cushioning the pressure.

The suspension bridges were every bit as thrilling as I had heard they would be, swinging high above twisting canyons, creaking alarmingly with every step.

'Don't go on the bridges when there's a mule train crossing,' Kami warned us. 'You can get butted over the edge if they freak out.'

Here in the highlands, with access to mountain rivers and streams, the famine was less intense. The meltwater from glaciers was sustaining the people even though it had barely rained for two years. The terraces were alive with barley and spinach and potato crops.

'This is like Shangri-La compared to the zone around the camp,' Tashi said. 'The people here are blessed.'

Later, we stopped to share some tea from our flask, sitting in the forest and enjoying the flash of colour as bee-eaters flitted amongst the trees. The air was dense with the sweet smell of nectar.

'So different to Tibet,' Tashi laughed.

I thought of the stark beauty of Tashi's homeland. The vast grasslands and glittering lakes; the hundred-mile views and ever-busy wind.

If the monsoon continued to fail, would Nepal go the same way? Become a desert land like Tibet?

Later that afternoon we found three Australian trekkers, sitting by the track.

One of the women was sobbing.

'Just to warn you,' her friend said, 'we were robbed last night. A gang of bandits burst into our lodge and ransacked our rooms.'

'Seriously?' I asked. I had never heard of such a thing happening in Nepal.

Kami and Shreeya looked at each other, absolutely horrified.

'Anyone hurt?' Alex asked.

'No. But if we'd resisted, things could have got nasty.'

'We just want to go home,' the woman said. 'Get out of this place.'

'How can this happen?' her friend asked. 'I always thought Nepal was a peaceful, welcoming country.'

'It is,' Kami said, his voice thick with emotion. 'The people are kind. But underneath are problems and stresses like anywhere else.'

Tashi flashed me a look. We knew all about those.

'There's no one in charge any more,' Alex told them. 'So it's going to take a while before things calm down.'

'One of the bandits said something strange,' one of the women told us. 'He said, *"Killer storm is coming"*. What do you think he meant?'

Alex frowned. 'I don't think he was talking about the weather.'

There was a silence while we pondered his words. Then Kami spoke: 'Contact my friend in Lukla,' he told the ladies. 'They will make sure you are safe.'

He gave them the name of a good friend, and instructions on how to find them in the town.

'Can we help you with anything else?' Alex asked. 'What do you need?'

The Australian women used our mobile phones to call home and borrowed a thousand dollars from Alex.

'We'll wait in Lukla until we hear things have calmed down in Kathmandu,' they said. 'Thank you so much for your help.'

We watched them walk away. Three disillusioned, scared trekkers whose Base Camp dream was over.

'I don't want to be ashamed of my country,' Shreeya said. 'Those bandits should be punished.'

'The local people won't let them get away with it,' Kami said. 'If the trekkers stop coming they will starve, just like the people in the lowlands.'

That night we stayed in an ancient lodge in Monjo. The earthquake had warped the beams of the building so that the whole place felt twisted out of shape. The wooden window surrounds were also bent, enough that the wind whistled through the gaps.

Shreeya didn't join us for supper.

'She keeps being sick,' Kami said. 'It must be the altitude.' He took her some potato soup but she couldn't eat it.

Tashi and I had a room right next to the alley – the main drag through the hamlet.

Local boys raced horses late into the night, hooves clattering on the cobbles as they shot down the hill.

When the boys finished their reckless races, a couple of local tomcats took up the challenge of keeping us awake, howling indignantly at each other then screaming with rage as they fought.

'It's quieter in Kathmandu,' Tashi complained, pulling a blanket over her head.

The trek continued at a more urgent pace, the mountain scenery becoming increasingly spectacular with every twist and turn of the valleys.

I found myself childishly excited at every new peak we saw.

Pumori. Lhotse. Nuptse.

I spent hours poring over the map, wanting to know and name every summit.

'There's a view of Everest later this morning,' Alex told us.

We gathered in a forest glade, happy to have a break from the one-step-after-another routine of the trek.

'It's just the tip you can see,' Kami said. 'But spectacular anyway.'

It was a stunningly clear day. Perfect visibility allowed us to see the top section of Everest's South-West Face.

'How many miles away are we, as the crow flies?' I asked Alex.

'Maybe thirty,' he guessed.

It was an amazing thought. Even at thirty miles' distance we could easily notice features on the ridge. I could make out the famous Hillary Step – the twenty-metre-high notch bitten out of the ridgeline – which was a last test on the way to the top.

We took dozens of photographs.

Just as we were about to head off, the Russian girl Zhanna arrived with a Nepali man we hadn't previously met.

'I thought you weren't going to trek?' Tashi exclaimed.

'I know,' Zhanna sighed. 'My father is going to go crazy.

But now I'm here I can't resist going to Base Camp. This is Dawa by the way. We found him! Anisa had to stay back in Lukla – she wasn't well.'

We nodded a hello.

Zhanna turned, her gaze fixed on Everest. I saw a tear slip down her cheek.

'It's beautiful,' she said. 'Almost too beautiful to climb.'

She stood there for ages, transfixed by the vision of Everest. In the end, her friend had to pull her away.

Namche Bazaar was a great landmark to reach, the most famous of the market towns on the way to Everest. We arrived mid-afternoon, footsore and tired after a three-hour climb up the valley wall. Now, standing at a high vantage point, we had the whole of the town laid out before us, the colourful buildings contouring up the sides of the hill.

'Namche wouldn't exist if it weren't for Everest,' Alex said. 'The whole thing has grown up to service trekkers and climbers.'

It was true that the town was a kind of mountaineers' paradise, designed to give weary climbers everything they wanted, from pizza houses to health spas. Hot chocolate with whipped cream was on offer in many cafes. Travel agencies advertised treks to far-flung parts of Nepal.

We found a general store and stocked up with trekking food. Salted peanuts and dried pineapple strips were the favourite choices.

'My earnings are down seventy per cent this year,' the store boss told us. 'If things carry on like this, I'm going back to India.'

Tashi was delighted to find Tibetan traders camping in the lower part of the town, men and women who had trekked over the high passes of the Himalaya, carrying huge loads of lapis and jade jewellery, clothing and cheap Chinese hooch.

'I can catch up with the news,' she said. We sat with the traders in their ramshackle yak-hide tent and shared butter tea. The Tibetans were cautious to begin with, perhaps suspecting Tashi was a Chinese spy, but once they got the measure of her they were happy to talk.

'The Chinese are controlling the high passes like never before,' one of the Tibetan women said. 'We have to cross the mountains in the night; take more risks.'

I thought of the terrible incident that had occurred some years before; a group of Tibetan pilgrims shot at by a Chinese patrol as they crossed a high pass.

'They are even spying here in Nepal,' another told us.

'Government officials posing as traders. They collect information on the numbers of Nepali troops, the locations of army camps.'

Tashi told the traders her story, how her family had been targeted by Chinese officials, their ancestral grazing lands cordoned off for mining, their herds condemned on the flimsiest of excuses.

'We had to escape into Nepal,' she concluded. 'Make our lives here – at least for the time being. But we'll be back living in Tibet as soon as we can.'

The traders nodded. They knew the mindset of refugees. They never regarded their exile as permanent. The longing to return to their heritage, to the crisp air and rolling hills of their Tibetan homeland, would never diminish.

'You will go back,' a lady trader with a gorgeous smile told Tashi. 'We all will. When our land is our own once more.'

In the minds of these courageous people there was no doubt that Tibet would, one day, be free again.

That first night in Namche was the night we learned just how serious things had become down in Kathmandu. Like many lodges on the Everest trail, our accommodation had a widescreen TV mounted on the wall of the dining room.

Normally, Nepali TV showed Bollywood movies, or repeats of classic football matches. That night was different, with images of buildings in flames, mobs running in the streets.

'Where's that?' Tashi asked. 'Syria? Iraq?'

'It's Kathmandu,' Kami said grimly. 'They're destroying the government buildings.'

We watched, astonished and dismayed, as the rioting gang took control of the streets.

Flames filled the screen. The biggest of the temples in Barkhor Square was on fire. The elegant wooden structure that had stood for a thousand years was now burning down on prime-time television. Yards away, a tear-gas grenade spewed out white smoke.

A police jeep drove at crazy speed into a barricade of burning tyres.

'There's so much anger,' Kami said sadly. 'The people can't take any more.'

The television footage continued for a further ten minutes or so then cut abruptly. A mob of men appeared briefly in front of the camera then it flickered to a distorted fuzz of lines.

'They've invaded the television studio,' Alex said. 'We won't be seeing any more from Kathmandu for a while.'

We talked late into the night, wondering what magical intervention could save Nepal.

'How about the Dalai Lama?' Tashi said. 'The country needs someone to lead it out of this misery.'

It was a wonderful thought. Beautifully simple. And totally impossible to imagine. Nepal's northern neighbour, China, would fight tooth and nail against such a move. The spiritual leader of the Tibetan people was public enemy number one for the autocratic leaders of Beijing.

'We are a rudderless ship,' Kami said. 'Heading for the rocks.'

Kami and Alex took us on a special trek the next day, to see a monument to a friend who had been with them on their previous Everest trip.

A huge yak train laden with expedition barrels was lumbering ahead of us, their bells clunking rhythmically as they climbed.

Alex checked his altimeter.

'We just reached 4,000 metres,' he said.

He didn't need to remind us. Our bodies were feeling it. Each of us had the constant headaches that come with altitude adjustment.

The landscape changed dramatically as we trekked up the side of a hill, tropical forests giving way to alpine meadows and high grasslands carpeted with tiny flowers.

Later, on a high pass next to a glacier, we found the beautiful stone memorial, one of the many dozens of shrines that line the route to Base Camp.

I saw the expression on Kami's face change, a look of intense sadness passing across it.

Alex bit his lip. I could see he was trying to hold it together.

It was a monument to Sasha, the journalist who had accompanied Alex and Kami on their first Everest expedition. She had been killed in an avalanche while saving Kami's life.

Sasha had uncovered the truth about Alex's cynical attempt to lie about reaching Everest's summit, and although Kami and Alex had since become reconciled, the emotional wounds were still raw.

Kami gently brushed snow off the metal plaque that bore Sasha's name and date of birth.

'This is the first time I've seen it,' Alex said.

He stood next to Kami. Both of them had tears in their eyes.

'She was special,' Kami said. 'I think of her every day.'

'You wouldn't be here if it wasn't for her,' Alex added.

I felt awkward standing with them. Their shared grief was an intensely private moment.

Kami placed a dried flower on the cairn, then said a series of prayers with the shrine bell cradled in his hands. Alex lit a candle and put it next to the flower.

Kami finished with a line of English.

'Compassion and prayer will help us to bring Sasha to a new life,' he said. 'Through the intervention of the gods she will be reincarnated and reborn into a life of happiness and joy.'

He rang the shrine bell, and I could see he was savouring the sound as it rang out across the hillside.

When I turned I found that a group of mountaineers had gathered behind us to watch the little ceremony. They were as moved by it as I was.

'Talking about reincarnation would feel unreal back in England,' I told Tashi. 'Isn't it strange that here it feels totally natural?'

'It's the spirit of the place,' Tashi said, gesturing to the breathtaking peaks that surrounded us. 'The mountains inspire spirituality, that's why people feel good when they climb. Nobody could be cynical with this view before them.'

Shreeya was definitely the weakest member of our team. She had been feeling sick since the start of the trek and frequently needed to rest on the trail.

At Namche Bazaar she felt worse, hardly eating and spending long hours sleeping in the lodge. We thought it was the thin air taking effect until Shreeya made an announcement at breakfast one day.

'We're going to have a baby,' she said proudly. 'If the gods allow.'

Kami patted Shreeya's belly and she beamed with excitement.

'Way to go, Shreeya!' Alex cried. We clustered round the happy couple for a group hug.

'I thought it was the altitude,' Shreeya laughed. 'But it turned out it was something much nicer.'

'It is the second miracle of my life,' Kami exclaimed, his expression radiant. 'Something I could only dream of.'

'Will you stay with us for the rest of the trek?' Tashi asked.

'I'll keep going,' Shreeya said. 'I asked a doctor if it's OK and she said yes. There's no reason why not so long as I am acclimatised.'

'I've sent a message to my family,' Kami added. 'After Base Camp we will return to my village and wait for the baby to arrive.'

Later, as the evening light became soft, Tashi and I saw Kami and Shreeya go to the small shrine next to the lodge. It was garlanded with fresh marigolds and we watched as Kami scattered some handfuls of rice about the rock that made up the centrepiece.

'We are blessed,' Kami said. 'The shrine bell has protected us and we are thanking the gods.'

'New life is coming,' Shreeya said. 'New life is growing inside me. We are praying that our child will know love and peace.'

'So many good things happening,' Tashi said later. 'And so many bad. On the one hand Kami and Shreeya's beautiful news. On the other, the riots, the famine. It can mess with your mind if you think about it too much.'

'I know what you mean,' I said, staring into space.

We tried to sleep but a series of small earth tremors rocked the lodge. They were tiny earthquakes, the sort that happen hundreds of times a year across the Himalaya. The beams above our head creaked. The glass in the windows flexed. A trekking book fell off the top of my rucksack.

Nothing dramatic, but unsettling nevertheless.

The local dogs started howling in the fields outside.

One week to Base Camp. The journey had already been a richer experience than we could have imagined.

CHAPTER 4

The following day started in the most unexpected way. A young boy came to the lodge as we ate breakfast and asked a question.

'Do you want to see a yeti skull?'

'A *real* yeti skull?' Alex smiled.

'Yes, sir. One hundred per cent guaranteed yeti, sir, you will see! I take you to the monastery at Khumjung. You will love the yeti, sir!'

The boy had made a good pitch and he was only asking for a handful of coins to take us to the mysterious relic. We finished our breakfast and followed him out into the town. He led us past local shacks where porters were eating smoked meat and dumplings, past stone corrals where yaks had been haltered overnight.

The smells were rich in the crisp early morning air.

Then we climbed. Up a precipitous heather-covered hill, which pushed our lungs to the limit. We were still only partly acclimatised and an attempt to follow the boy's dizzying pace left me gasping for breath with stars floating in front of my eyes.

The views became even more inspiring; the vast sentinel peak of Kongde Ri revealed itself as a cloud moved aside.

We crossed a pass and found the monastery, built into the shadow of a nearby cliff.

Zhanna was there as well, waiting in the courtyard for the temple to open up. She had her friend Dawa with her.

'Are you here for the yeti?' she asked excitedly.

The stooped old lama was summoned from his rest. He fussed his saffron and purple robes into position, greeted us with a dignified speech in Nepali, then explained in English that he would conduct the morning prayers before we could see the yeti skull.

'Photos are permitted,' he said. 'But video is forbidden.'

He opened a book of parchment and began to chant, pausing occasionally as his broken spectacles slipped down.

We sat cross-legged on cushions, enjoying the heady atmosphere of the monastery and the sweet smell of incense wafting from a burner. The walls were decorated with intricate scenes depicting Buddhist sutras. Devils and demons raced in and out of the shadows.

The old man seemed to appreciate the audience, looking up frequently to make sure we were paying attention.

After the ceremony the old lama cut to the chase.

'Now! The relic!' he exclaimed.

We gathered round a box covered with a yellow and red silk cloth, which he pulled back with a flourish.

Behind a glass screen we saw a hairy cone, similar in size and appearance to a big coconut.

Alex's eyebrows shot skywards. Zhanna snorted with laughter, turning it into a strangled cough.

I was close to cracking up myself. It really didn't look very yeti-like at all, more like cowhide that had been stretched into an elongated football.

'The mystery of this artefact goes back 100 years,' the lama said. 'Tests have proved that it does not belong to any living … '

The door suddenly crashed open.

A group of soldiers burst in.

'Good morning,' one of them said. His speech was slurred.

I noticed that Zhanna's Nepali friend Dawa pulled her

quickly back into the shadows, standing in front of her in a protective stance.

I could smell the alcohol on the soldier's breath. His men were swaying on their feet, their eyes red.

'Give me the key!' the soldier said to the lama. He nodded to the corner of the temple.

I guessed what he was referring to – a donation box for visitors, a metal cash box mounted on a solid concrete plinth. It was protected by a hefty-looking padlock.

'You have no right to be here,' the lama said, his voice trembling. 'This is a place of peace.'

The soldier yanked at the holy man's robe, pulling a chain up around his neck. A silver key glinted in the temple candlelight.

A vicious tug saw the key in the man's hand.

'That money belongs to the monastery,' the lama said.

At that moment, a dozen men came through the door. Word of the army raid had spread like lightning through the town and a group of monks had arrived, strong-looking young men who moved in quickly to stand by the side of the lama.

The soldier took out a pistol and brandished the gun at the youths.

One of the young monks stepped forward.

'Go now,' he said. 'Or we'll throw you out.'

The soldiers looked to their leader. He swayed drunkenly for a few moments, obviously unsure what to do. He kicked out at one of the monks.

'We're not leaving without the money,' he said.

Two or three of the monks moved in front of the cash box.

The stand-off looked like it was about to get extremely ugly.

'Excuse me!' came a voice from behind us.

We turned in surprise.

It was Zhanna.

She stepped towards the confrontation, smiling pleasantly. Her friend Dawa held her back for a moment but she shrugged him away.

'It's OK,' I heard her mutter. 'I've got an idea.'

Her protector looked uncertain, hesitating for a critical second as Zhanna moved confidently towards the soldier.

'If I can make that key disappear by magic,' Zhanna said, 'will you take your men away?'

The soldier blinked. 'What are you talking about?'

Tashi gave me a quizzical look.

'Give me the key,' Zhanna said. She smiled reassuringly.

The man paused. The mood in the temple had already

shifted. Zhanna was such an imposing personality, everyone was curious to know what on earth she was up to.

'Give me the key, please,' she repeated.

One of the soldiers laughed and urged the boss to do it. He handed over the key.

Zhanna put the tiny silver key in her hand. She slowly closed her fist.

'Alakazam!' she cried suddenly, making everyone start.

She blew on it with a theatrical flourish, then opened her hand once again.

The key was gone.

The soldiers' eyes widened.

'Watch!' Zhanna said. She reached forward and plucked the key from behind the holy man's left ear.

The old lama chuckled in amazement. A ripple of nervous laughter ran around the temple.

Zhanna flexed her fingers, moving her hand upwards in an abrupt movement.

'Alakazam!' she cried once more.

The key vanished again. This time she seemed to pull it from the old lama's nose. It was done so well that a small round of applause broke out.

'One last time!' she cried.

Once again the key disappeared. Zhanna bowed and

walked back to join her friend, who seemed mightily relieved the impromptu show had ended.

The lama clapped his hands.

'Enough! Now, go!' he ordered the soldiers.

Zhanna's display had taken all the aggression out of the confrontation. The soldiers turned and left, still talking animatedly about the tricks.

The rest of us clustered around Zhanna.

'You turned that around brilliantly!' Alex said.

'No problem,' she replied. 'It was a good chance to practise my magic.'

The lama approached. 'I must thank you,' he said. 'And also kindly request that you return my key.'

'Key?' Zhanna said, totally deadpan. 'Do you mean the one in Tashi's pocket?'

Tashi found the key. We burst into laughter and a spontaneous round of applause.

Zhanna and her friend left the temple. The show was over.

We chatted about the incident on the trek back to Namche, all of us struck by the bizarre but courageous way Zhanna had dealt with the situation.

'What a character,' Tashi said. 'She's something else.'

'She was certainly icy calm,' Alex said with a laugh.

'She won't get fazed by the trek to Base Camp, that's for sure.'

We talked about the soldiers, wondering how they could stoop so low as to try and rob a monastery.

'It's shocking,' Tashi said. 'Such a thing would never happen in Tibet.'

'The people are losing their respect for religion,' Kami agreed. 'Everything is falling apart in Nepal.'

We had one more acclimatisation day in Namche. Long hours spent drinking gallons of tea and eating apple pie. There was a palpable sense of impatience amongst our little team.

'I want to get back on the trail,' Kami said as we played our umpteenth game of chess together in the lodge. 'The higher we go, the more I feel a sense of peace.'

His words felt natural at the time. Only later would I see the irony loaded within them.

Porridge and chapattis were served at dawn.

We grabbed our trekking poles and hit the trail.

The first part of the trail was a breathtaking traverse. The path hugged the side of a mountain spur, passing beneath the glowering scrutiny of the ferocious Hindu gods painted on to the cliffs.

We approached the big hill that leads up to the monastery of Tengboche, a three-hour ascent with a fearsome
reputation.

The climb began down by the river, crossing a suspension
bridge, low enough to leave us soaked with spray.

'My first shower in a week!' Kami laughed.

We stopped at a small shack for lunch, and a discussion
kicked off. Alex had been brooding for a few days but I was
still surprised when he said:

'I'm beginning to think this might not be the right time
to be here. How about we talk about heading back down?'

There was a stunned silence, then Kami spoke.

'We cannot go back,' he said passionately. 'It would be
a betrayal of everything this trek is about. This journey
is about the shrine bell, to make a prayer at Base Camp.
A prayer that will bring the monsoon back to Nepal. If we
give up, we will be giving up on millions of people.'

Tashi and I agreed. It didn't make sense to try and return
to Kathmandu. Even with incidents like the bandits we
had heard about and the drunken soldiers we had encoun-
tered, it still felt safer to be up here in the mountain valleys
than down in the chaos of Kathmandu.

'We'll never know if Kami's prayer is going to work

unless we keep going to Base Camp,' Tashi said. 'Everyone OK with that?'

Alex shrugged. 'I guess.'

So it was resolved. Base Camp it was, but I could see that Alex was still troubled by the situation.

Gorak Shep was our next overnight stop. Three windswept lodges built along the banks of an ancient dried-out lake. The cosy rooms of lower altitudes were now little more than a fond memory. Tashi and I were shown into a bare concrete cell that wouldn't have looked out of place in a Siberian Gulag.

The heater in the lodge restaurant was fired up at 7 p.m. A massive steel drum into which combustible waste of all descriptions was loaded, along with the occasional wooden log.

After a couple of false starts when it belched out noxious fumes, the stove cranked up to a volcanic level of warmth which won it a fan club of grateful heat seekers intent on drying off newly washed socks or just holding chilly fingers towards the glow.

We ordered dumplings and fried eggs, daubing them in oceans of tomato sauce to disguise the earthy farmyard taste of the yak fat in which they'd been cooked.

'Kami? Kami!'

A cry went up from one of the lodge workers. We turned in surprise.

Kami stood, staring uncertainly at the worker for a beat or two.

'Nima?'

Then a big smile washed over both of them and they embraced.

It was Nima, a Sherpa friend of Kami's who had been alongside him on Alex's expedition. I had stumbled across him a couple of years earlier on my solo journey to find Kami, a troubling encounter which left me worrying about his future.

'Boss?' Nima stepped towards Alex, hugging him less warmly.

The time I had met him, this young man – Nima – had been in a very dark place. Seriously injured by frostbite, his wounds had become infected and he was struggling to find work. He had become one of the many Sherpas whose lives are effectively destroyed by the mountain, hanging around in sleazy bars, begging drinks from passers-by in return for recounting an Everest tale or two.

'Let me see your hands?' Kami asked.

The fingers were gone but the stumps were healed.

'You helped me,' Nima said, gesturing my way with a smile. I was pleased he remembered the medical attention I'd given him.

Nima sat with us to share the food. Kami explained the story of his injuries, how the two of them had been stranded in a crevasse in the Icefall after a filming session; the dropped climbing gear that had condemned Nima to hours in the frozen tomb.

'It was my mistake,' Kami said.

'Yes, and for a long time I blamed you,' Nima said. 'Then I went to a monastery for six months and the anger left me.'

'It was my fault,' Alex said. He gave Nima a steady look. 'I should have made sure you guys got out of the crevasse without any problems. I'm sorry, Nima.'

Nima nodded graciously. It was encouraging to see how well he was doing. He couldn't rebuild his fingers, but he could rebuild his life.

From Gorak Shep the trail kept to the side of the glacier, a switchback path that climbed and descended with each twist and turn of the terrain. It was dangerous ground, the track often crossing fragile slopes that were liable to slide away beneath the weight of a trekker.

A wary eye was necessary for tumbling boulders from

above. The mountain shed stones in a continuous process of erosion. Small streams of meltwater ran across the track.

We passed a dead yak. Vultures had picked the flesh from the bones.

One mile from Base Camp the path took an abrupt right fork, moving out on to the glacier itself. The trail was still far from flat, weaving a route across fractured terrain.

'Slow down, Ryan!' Tashi called, laughing. 'You're like a kid on the way to a party!'

It was true – I was in a hurry to arrive. Coming to Base Camp here on the Nepali side had been a dream for as long as I could remember.

As I waited for her to catch up, I saw that Zhanna Kuzkin and her friend were trekking just behind us. Zhanna was in front, powering up the ice slopes with a determined look on her face, her trekking poles almost a blur.

'She's strong,' Tashi said. 'No doubt about that.'

'The power of youth,' I agreed. 'I reckon she could summit if she wanted.'

We had reached the viewpoint from which the whole of Base Camp could be seen. It was a sight to stir the blood. Hundreds of tents spread out, flags fluttering proudly in the wind, satellite dishes and radio masts being erected even as we watched.

Tashi and I gave each other a huge hug. As usual, she had been brilliant all the way through the trek.

The smell of cooking wafted from the catering tents, the aroma of freshly brewed coffee and frying bacon tantalising in the morning air.

A cousin of Kami's was working as a porter for a Spanish team of climbers. He invited us for breakfast and we found ourselves sitting in a roomy tent with a plate of eggs and beans and a steaming mug of tea.

'You made it, Kami,' Shreeya said.

'We're all proud of you,' Alex added.

Kami and I embraced. 'Well done, my friend,' he told me, simply.

'We need to build a cairn.' Kami gazed at the fluttering prayer flags all around us, tears in his eyes. 'It's time for a puja.'

'Isn't that just for people who are planning to go to the top?' Tashi asked.

'Not at all,' Kami replied. 'It's to thank the gods for all the good things in our lives. And to pray for the monsoon to return.'

We all helped to haul stones off the glacier and built a nicely shaped cairn. Prayer flags were raised on a pole above it.

A holy man was in residence at Base Camp. Virtually every team holds a puja ceremony so he was in constant demand.

We paid a small sum to persuade him to come along.

The lama opened a battered leather book with trembling hands. Following ancient inscriptions on the page with his finger, he began to mutter the many prayers and sutras that would make the puja complete.

We stood in a circle around him, each of us enjoying it in our own way.

At the close, threads of red cotton were produced. The lama muttered some words over them then tied them one by one around our necks to confirm we had participated.

'The mountain has blessed you,' he said, simply.

At that point we should have turned round and trekked back out.

Technically, we weren't supposed to spend the night at Base Camp. Only those who have a climbing permit for Everest are allowed to stay. But Kami had plenty of Sherpa friends at the camp and they were more than happy to bend the rules and lend us some tents.

We had a great party that night. The Sherpas rigged up some speakers in the mess tent and a good few bottles of beer were cracked open. Music was blaring across the glacier until the early hours. There were some legendary Sherpa climbers among the partygoers, including one who had been sixteen times to the summit.

'Do you get tired of coming back to Everest?' I asked him.

'The mountain is different every time,' he said. 'It changes every single season.'

'Does it get easier?' Tashi asked him.

'Never!' he exclaimed. 'No matter how many times a climber summits, it's still the ultimate challenge.'

The party ended and our little team dispersed in fine spirits, if a little unsteady on our feet.

Tashi and I retreated to our tent, peeling up the zip and creating a mini plume of ice crystals in the glow of our head torches.

'I forgot how tiring altitude is,' I said.

My head felt like it was packed with cotton wool.

I was asleep as soon as my head hit the pillow.

It didn't last long.

The attack began at dawn.

Shouting on the glacier.

At first I thought I was imagining it. I rolled over in my sleeping bag and pulled the hood tight around my head.

More shouts – definitely real. In my hazy early morning state I figured it might be another puja ceremony; sometimes they get pretty rowdy.

I sat up. Scratched my head.

A puja? At dawn?

There's no such thing. An explosion shocked the air, the retort echoing backwards and forwards on the valley walls.

Was that a gunshot?

Tashi woke.

'What's happening?' she murmured. 'Was that a gun?'

'Sounded like one.'

The shouts intensified. The sound of something breaking reached us. I heard a Western woman's voice yelling 'Come out of your tents. Come out now!'

'I'll go and check,' I said. Tashi shrugged and rolled back over. I guess she thought it was someone having a joke or messing around.

I pulled on my warm gear and unzipped the tent.

The first thing I saw was half a dozen men attacking the main communications mast. They were smashing at the base of the metal tower with ice axes and rocks. I blinked in surprise. A handful of Sherpa guys approached them but quickly moved back when guns were pulled out.

The mast fell with a crash of splintered metal.

Two climbers from a nearby team came running past.

'We're under attack! Like Nanga Parbat. Run, while you still can.'

Like Nanga Parbat? A terror attack?

I thought back to the events they were referring to. The killings at Nanga Parbat Base Camp in 2013 had shaken the mountaineering world to its core. Terrorists had pulled climbers from their tents and slaughtered eleven in cold blood. Only two people survived.

Now terror had come to Everest.

A German was pulled from his tent. The attackers beat him.

I ducked behind a boulder, peeping over as icy daggers of fear pricked my spine. Out of the gloom came a new figure, an imposing woman with long plaits of platinum-blonde hair. She was dressed in military fatigues, an assault rifle held confidently in her hands.

'Where is Zhanna Kuzkin? Where is her tent?' she hissed at a hapless climber.

She pointed her gun at the man's face and he gestured towards the Russian camp, just a stone's throw from our own.

The attackers moved towards it. It seemed that Zhanna was their main target.

A twelve-year-old girl with the richest father in the world.

It wasn't difficult to work out what this was about.

I thought about Tashi – about Shreeya, pregnant and even more vulnerable. I knew we had to act fast. I ran across the moraine and shook the top of the tent.

'Tashi! Get your boots on. We have to get out of here.'

I rattled the other tents. Alex emerged. Kami and Shreeya looked out, their faces ashen.

'What's happening?' Alex asked. He rubbed sleep from his eyes.

Just twenty metres from our position a new gang of invaders came into view. They were wild-looking men, some bearded, some dressed in military clothing. They began dragging more climbers from their tents, threatening them with their guns when they objected. One of them was Zhanna's friend Dawa.

'You know Zhanna?' they said. 'Where is she?'

Dawa threw a punch. He was beaten to the ground, his leg twisting awkwardly as he fell.

'There's no time to pack,' I told the others. 'Let's get out of here.'

'What about Zhanna?' Tashi said urgently. 'We should try and help her.'

We stared at Zhanna's camp, now being ransacked by more than forty attackers, desperate to find their quarry.

The tall blonde woman – evidently a leader of some sort – was barking instructions.

'Nothing we can do,' Alex said decisively.

'But … ' I began. It felt so wrong to abandon Zhanna.

Her camp was already overrun.

Within seconds the others were ready.

'This way!' Alex said. We hurried away from our camp, heading down a slope into a natural gully that would give us some cover. Alex kept a punishing pace, leading us ever faster to the south. I couldn't help fearing that a volley of bullets might follow us at any moment.

We kept moving, down in that hollow, putting space between the attackers and us. Halfway down the strip we stopped; we heard shouting ahead.

'There's more than one group of attackers,' Tashi whispered. We watched cautiously, using the undulating terrain for cover, as more climbers were pulled from their tents at gunpoint.

'The girl? The girl?' the raiders shouted.

'They can't find Zhanna,' Alex whispered.

'Someone might have alerted her,' Tashi said. 'Maybe the attackers were seen coming into camp.'

We raised our heads as high as we dared above the rocks, trying to get a fix on what was happening. But the terrorists were herding people away from us and we couldn't see clearly.

'No time to lose,' Alex urged. 'We need to get out while things are in a state of confusion.'

We continued south but things got slow. The glacier was split with crevasses that were too big to jump. We had to zigzag to find a way through.

A tent loomed up. A medical centre run by a charity. We crouched down in a small crevasse, watching from a safe distance as several of the terrorists looted the drugs from inside.

'These men are nothing but thieves,' Alex whispered. 'They're totally undisciplined.'

The men stuffed their spoils in rucksacks and marched briskly off towards the middle of the camp. We continued, and after twenty minutes of progress we found a place where huge boulders were scattered on the ice. We hid behind one of the bigger rocks, Tashi peeking out to see what was happening.

'There are three armed men,' she whispered. 'They've sealed the only way out.'

The single path out of Base Camp was under guard.

A Sherpa ran up to the attackers, began to argue with them. He was pushed off balance then struck with the butt of a gun as he fell.

He limped away, swearing at the invaders, his arm hanging at a strange angle. Tashi's face was white.

'These people are animals,' she said. 'I think they just broke that man's arm.'

We heard more screaming back in the main camp area.

The situation was deteriorating fast.

'We could try going without the path,' Kami whispered. 'Just head south on the glacier?'

'That's not an option,' Alex replied. 'We won't make it.'

I had to agree with Alex. The glacier got a lot more dangerous as it flowed down the valley.

Trying to blaze a new trail across it could prove lethal. Or even impossible. Four miles of tortured ice stood between us and the nearest safe refuge at Gorak Shep. The terrain was packed with hazards that could swallow us up in the blink of an eye.

Besides, the terrorists would spot us easily.

'Can we get over one of the valley walls?' Tashi asked.

We stared at the vertical ramparts that surrounded us. Two serious mountains turned this place into a natural dead end: Pumori loomed on one side, Nuptse on the other.

Hanging glaciers threatened both sides. There was no

realistic trail.

Base Camp was a perfect trap.

'I think we've been spotted,' Kami hissed.

We heard a shout. The tall blonde woman dressed in combat clothes was fast approaching with a group of men.

CHAPTER 5

'Come out!' she cried. 'Hands where we can see them.'

Her voice was harsh, the accent guttural.

We moved into view, arms raised high.

'Where can I find Zhanna Kuzkin?' she asked.

Alex stepped forward.

'Who's asking?' he said. I had to admire his nerve.

'They call me Viking,' the terrorist said. 'I've been told your team have been hanging out with Zhanna. So you'd better tell us what you know. Anyone here got a problem with that?'

'Yeah, as it happens,' Alex said. 'I do.'

Viking's eyes glittered.

'And you are?'

'An American citizen who doesn't appreciate being pushed around,' Alex said.

'Well excuse me,' Viking replied sarcastically. 'I didn't realise you were an *American citizen*! That changes everything. Why don't I just call you up a limousine to take you home to mommy?'

Her team of thugs laughed.

'Where is she?' she snapped. 'Where is the girl?'

We were silent.

Viking pushed past her bodyguard and stood face-to-face with Alex.

'What's your name?' she asked.

'Alex Brennan. Why don't you let the women go?' Alex said steadily. He nodded to Shreeya and Tashi. 'And the Nepali nationals. I imagine you've got no argument with them.'

'All I want,' Viking declared, 'is to find Anatoly Kuzkin's daughter.'

'You're a monster,' Alex spat.

'And you are a typical big-mouthed American,' Viking said. She shoved Alex in the chest and for a brief moment his fists clenched and I saw fight in his eyes.

I pulled him back.

'Leave it,' I said. I had a terrible feeling that Viking

would shoot him.

The terror leader jabbed Alex hard in the chest with the barrel of her weapon. He cried out, doubling up.

'You come with us,' Viking said.

We followed instructions, trekking in single file up the trail that led back to the central zone of Base Camp.

Alex stumbled along, clutching his ribs.

Viking's men guarded us, one on one. They seemed a mixed bunch. Some looked Eastern European, some looked Asian. They didn't have a uniform as such, but lots of them were wearing bits and pieces of military clothing.

The guns were real enough. Assault rifles of various types.

Onwards we marched, losing all the valuable ground we had gained, the scowling terrorists on either side of us, their stony-faced leader at the rear.

My spine tingled. I tried to recall what had happened at Nanga Parbat.

Summary executions. Random shootings. Climbers from all over the world, killed by a terror group whose motives were never made clear.

'You think they're going to shoot us?' I whispered to Kami.

'They want Zhanna,' he said. 'But I guess anything can happen.'

A crowd was growing. Close to the wreckage of the radio mast the inhabitants of Base Camp were being herded together.

It was an incredible sight. A thousand climbers in a single huddle, fear written across every face. I heard comments from all sides as we were marched through the masses.

'*They can't kill us all,*' one said.

'*We should attack them,*' muttered another.

The blonde giant got a briefing from one of her men. I was close enough to hear him say their search had failed.

Viking stood on a rock. One of her team stood filming her and I saw he had a satellite transmitter connected to his camera. She raised a megaphone and began to speak.

'My name is Viking,' she announced. 'And this is Operation Killer Storm. We're here to put things right. Show the world what Anatoly Kuzkin has been doing and force him to stop.'

Tashi flashed me a look and I immediately made the connection. The Australian trekkers had mentioned the same 'Killer Storm' some days earlier.

Now we knew what it meant.

Viking held a small hard drive aloft.

'We have tens of thousands of emails and files here, hacked from Kuzkin's personal computers. These prove beyond doubt that he is guilty of crimes against the planet. Hundreds of thousands of people are starving and dying because of his activities.'

She paused.

'So, all I need right now is Anatoly Kuzkin to come here. I need to talk to him face-to-face. We know he is somewhere in Nepal, but sadly my men did not manage to find him in the east of the country.'

A terrible silence befell the crowd.

The terrorist turned up the volume on the megaphone.

'But while Anatoly is not here right now, his daughter is. Zhanna! We know you are here. You must be hiding nearby. Come out!'

No one stirred.

'They want to use Zhanna as bait,' Tashi whispered to me.

'Evil,' I replied.

'Zhanna!' the megaphone blasted out. 'Come out now and I will let all your friends go free.'

The climbers looked around expectantly but I wasn't so sure Zhanna would give herself up. She would be terrified.

Viking turned back to the crowd of climbers.

'Why so silent? Are you feeling sorry for her father?' the terror leader went on. 'Don't waste your pity on Anatoly Kuzkin. Two monsoons have failed because of his mining operations – he's the reason this country is in such a mess.'

Tashi murmured. 'That's the article we saw,' she said.

'Zhanna?' she called into the megaphone, her voice more gentle. 'You have to be hiding somewhere on this glacier and I'm sure you can hear me.'

Her voice echoed around the walls of the valley, the natural acoustics projecting it over a huge distance.

'Come out, please. I promise you won't be harmed.'

One thousand climbers held their breath, but nothing stirred out on the glacier.

'OK,' Viking resumed her broadcast with the megaphone. She nodded at our group, glaring at Alex. 'Our American friend here has made it easy for me. His pig-headed attitude earlier means that it is he and his friends who will be kept hostage until you decide to make an appearance, Zhanna, and we get Anatoly to join us. The rest of you can leave. Get out of here!'

I got a hollow sensation deep in my guts. Tashi stared at me, her eyes wide with terror.

Someone shouted from the crowd.

'Can we go to our tents? Take our passports? Our valuables?'

'No!' Viking fired a burst of gunfire into the air. 'Move!

Move!'

Her men unshouldered their rifles, following her lead.

'Get out of here!'

A deafening crescendo erupted. Fifty rifles firing into the air.

The crowd of people didn't need to be told twice. A virtual stampede kicked off as every single climber and Sherpa at Base Camp turned on their heels and hurried for the trail to the south.

Every single climber that was, except for our small expedition and Zhanna's friend Dawa, who had been found hiding nearby.

We were surrounded by gunmen, marched out on to the glacier and over to a mess tent. Dawa was limping badly from the awkward tumble he'd taken during his earlier beating. He could walk, but only just.

The table and chairs were thrown out so we could all fit into the tent. Half a dozen men armed with AR-15 assault rifles guarded the entrance.

We found some space, huddled in a corner.

'Surrender your phones and walkie-talkies,' Viking ordered.

One of her men circulated amongst us, collecting the devices in a basket.

Then each of us was frisked in case we were hiding an extra phone.

'From now on you will not try to communicate with the outside world. You will stay in here until we give you orders.'

Viking walked away.

Tashi found a split in the wall of the tent.

'They're destroying our phones,' she whispered.

I peeked out of the gap and saw three of Viking's men crushing our devices into shards of plastic and metal.

Ten minutes later the generator that powered all the internet connections at Base Camp was also smashed to smithereens.

We were dead quiet for a while but it soon became clear that we could talk quietly without repercussions from the guards.

Alex huddled our little team together.

'I'm so sorry,' he whispered. 'It's my fault you've all been chosen. If I had just kept my big mouth shut for once ... '

'Don't feel bad,' Kami told him. 'You did the right thing challenging her.'

Dawa came over.

'We're going to have to work together,' he said. 'Strength

in numbers.'

'What about Zhanna? Where is she?' I asked him quietly.

'We had five minutes' warning that something was up,' Dawa whispered. 'A Sherpa friend of mine saw the terrorists coming up the glacier and raised the alarm. Zhanna had time to slip away.'

'Where is she now?' Alex whispered.

'I don't know. On her way down the valley, I hope.'

'Or maybe she's hiding out somewhere up here?' Tashi suggested.

'They'll find her if she is,' Alex said. 'They're going through every tent, looking behind every rock.'

'Don't underestimate Zhanna,' Dawa said.

'What about her dad? Will he try and organise a rescue if she does get caught?'

'Certainly,' Dawa replied. 'But think about the time it would take to get a team acclimatised – it could take days.'

'By which point … ' Alex said.

His statement hung in the air, reflecting the deep fears we all had.

'OK,' Kami asked. 'What's going to happen next?'

'I'm scared,' Shreeya whispered, her hands cradling her belly. 'Scared for my baby.'

'Maybe the government will send in special forces,'

Tashi said. 'Rescue us.'

'Nice idea,' Alex said, 'but there's no government in Kathmandu to make that happen.'

'How about the Americans?' Kami asked. 'They could do it.'

'No Western government is going to risk military action here,' Alex said. 'Apart from the obvious problem with the altitude, we're less than a mile from the Chinese border. Beijing could see it as an act of war.'

'Then we're going to rot here,' Dawa said. 'If Viking doesn't kill us first.'

'We'll come up with something,' I said. 'Look for an opportunity.'

The afternoon passed in a shocked state of silence. The guards came into the doorway of the tent from time to time, glowering aggressively at us.

'Watch them closely,' Alex whispered to me. 'They don't look well acclimatised.'

'Hey!' The leader of the watch waved his weapon at Alex. 'No talking!' he snarled.

I checked out the guards over the next hour and decided Alex was on to something. Three of the four looked ill. Two seemed oddly pale. One had the telltale blue tinge of oxygen deprivation on his lips.

'You're right,' I whispered back to Alex when I got a chance. 'They have come up too fast.'

'It might give us an opening,' Alex said.

The conversation fell away. Each of us trying to come up with a way through the problem. Then Dawa spoke.

'I have a gun hidden in my tent,' he said. 'After the riots in Lukla, I brought it along for security.'

'Where is it?' Alex asked.

'At the bottom of my sleeping bag.'

I wonder if I could sneak over and get the weapon, I thought. It was obvious that Dawa's leg was still too painful for him to walk far.

Later, Tashi and I peeked out of the flap in the tent. The guards were out of it, virtually falling asleep on their feet.

'These guys are total amateurs,' Alex observed.

We continued talking until midnight, falling into an uneasy sleep.

At 1 a.m. Tashi shook me awake.

'No one is watching the back of the tent,' she whispered. 'There's only one guy awake and he's out the front.'

My heart began to thump hard in my chest.

'There's just enough moonlight to see by,' she said. 'Let's try and get that weapon.'

I had to smile at her.

'Since when have you been a part of this?'

'Try and stop me,' she replied.

We pulled up the canvas, crawling on our bellies out on to the glacier, our entire bodies pumped up with adrenaline. We moved as stealthily as we could, hyperaware that even the smallest sound of rocks clunking against each other could alert a guard. Luckily the night was so cold the stones were iced together.

Twenty paces from the tent, we stood up. Using the protection of a wall of ice, we moved soundlessly and quickly away from our prison.

Dawa's tent was less than ten minutes away. We quickly entered and found the gun. I held it in my hand for a couple of seconds, astonished at its weight. Then I tucked it into my anorak pocket.

'Let's try some scavenging,' Tashi said, pointing to a huge tent nearby. 'We might find some warm clothing.'

We walked over and Tashi kept watch, checking for any guards that might be on patrol.

Stepping inside, I had to let my eyes adjust to the interior. A chink of moonlight was all I had to work with. Finally I saw that six equipment barrels were stacked there. Luckily for us, the terrorists hadn't looted them although they had opened them to see what was inside. It was the work of a few moments to find one containing the kit we needed, pulling out warm blankets and sleeping bags.

Tashi slipped in to join me. We put the gear in two rucksacks from the tent.

'See if you can find another sleeping bag,' Tashi whispered.

I reached into a final barrel, situated in the darkest shadows at the back of the tent.

And got the shock of my life.

Something moved inside.

'Don't shoot me!' said a familiar voice.

Zhanna rose like a jack-in-the-box from the barrel, her hands in the air.

'Zhanna!' Tashi gasped.

We helped her out of the barrel and she flung her arms around Tashi with a whispered squeal of delight.

'We should have known you'd be smart enough to hide away!' Tashi said.

'I've been so scared,' Zhanna said, her voice trembling. 'I could hear that woman shouting my name. Is she going to kill me? Tell me the truth!'

'How did they miss you?' I asked.

'I was curled up at the bottom of the barrel, a blanket on top of me,' Zhanna said. 'One of the men reached in but not deep enough. I guess he didn't think anyone would be small enough to hide there.'

'Clever move,' I said.

'What are you doing here?' she asked.

'Scavenging gear.'

We found some energy bars in a box, breaking them open to eat.

'Who is that woman? What will she do with me if she catches me?' Zhanna asked. Her eyes were wide with terror.

Tashi and I shared a look.

'Better not to think about that,' Tashi said.

'Maybe my father will do something,' she said urgently. She showed us the chunky watch on her wrist. 'I activated the emergency beacon on my watch. He will know my location to the nearest ten metres.'

'It's not just your father. The world will know about Killer Storm,' I told her. 'The terrorists have released hundreds of climbers and they'll be spreading the news.'

We talked for a while about possible escape routes for Zhanna but nothing seemed very certain and both Tashi and I felt that her safest option, at least for the next twenty-four hours, was to stay in her hiding spot.

'It's too lonely,' she protested. 'I've been going crazy on my own in here. Can't I go back with you? Maybe I can hide in your tent?'

'It's not going to work,' Tashi told her. 'Apart from anything else, there's no barrel to hide in.'

Zhanna's face crumpled. Tashi reached her arms around her and gave her the biggest hug ever.

I checked my watch.

'I'll go and see if the coast is clear.'

I sneaked back to the camp, dodging from boulder to boulder, only to find two guards had been positioned at the back of our tent. They were chatting quietly to each other, smoking cigarettes.

I swore beneath my breath. We had to get back into the tent by daybreak but these men would certainly see anyone trying to slip in.

Tashi and I would just have to wait until they moved.

I scrutinised them carefully. The guards were poorly dressed, obviously freezing. They were stamping their feet and flapping their arms about in an attempt to keep warm.

I reckoned they wouldn't resist long before they would seek some warmth. Meanwhile, I sneaked back to the supply tent and rejoined Zhanna and Tashi.

We scavenged some thick fleece blankets from a barrel

and built ourselves a snug little nest. Locked inside the fleeces we were warm as toast and we could talk quite safely as long as we whispered.

'How come you ended up here in Nepal?' Tashi asked Zhanna.

Zhanna took a deep breath.

CHAPTER 6

Zhanna's Story:
Three weeks earlier

Warm rain had been falling through the tropical night. The cicadas serenaded one another as Zhanna awoke. It was 5 a.m. and the young Russian girl felt her skin was sticky from the humid air. She yawned and stretched, listening for a while to the booming call of a night heron down by the pond. The sound was melodic but mournful, two notes repeated over and over.

Night in South East Asia. Raw nature, clustered on the other side of the shutters.

Zhanna liked that part of living in Singapore. Her

favourite hobby was photographing wildlife. It was the shopping malls and twenty-four-hour traffic jams that let the place down.

She heard a soft knock at the door. Anisa, the Indonesian maid, turned on the light and entered with a cup of tea, her kindly face wreathed in the perpetual smile that Zhanna had come to love.

'Time to get up,' she said. 'You don't want to keep the monkeys waiting.'

The monkeys. Long-tailed macaques. A teacher at Zhanna's school had told her about a place in the rain-forest where they might be seen at daybreak. Zhanna was so excited by the idea she had her camera ready on the bedside table.

She had waited two months for a weekend when her father, Anatoly, was at home.

'Monkeys?' he had grumbled. 'Why don't you watch them on the television?'

Zhanna dressed and hurried to the cosy warmth of the kitchen. Dawa, the Nepali driver and bodyguard to her father, was in there, a mug of coffee in his powerful hands. Zhanna loved to spend time with Dawa and Anisa; they were affectionate people, both from poor backgrounds, but in many ways happier in themselves than the rich people with whom Zhanna's father liked to socialise.

Anatoly came down late, his mobile phone ringing as he stuffed some toast into his mouth. Zhanna always thought her father had a hawkish look with his rather hooked nose, his narrow-set eyes misty blue, the colour of a distant mountain range.

'Idiot!' he exclaimed when he saw the identity of the caller on the screen.

Zhanna smiled weakly at Dawa as they waited in the hallway. She watched geckos dart for flies high on the walls, while Anatoly took his call in the office. He was yelling at whoever was on the line and Zhanna got a nauseous feeling in her belly as she heard the fury in his voice.

Dawa gave her a look, his eyebrows raised. They both knew how poisonous things could get when Anatoly was in a sour mood.

Finally Zhanna's father blundered out of the office.

'Right!' he exclaimed. 'Let's get on with it.'

Zhanna gave him her most winning smile. 'Can Anisa come?'

Anatoly scowled. 'I don't think so,' he snapped. 'There's work to do around the house.'

'Please, Papa.' Zhanna reached out for her father's hand. 'She hasn't had a day off in ages.'

Anatoly rolled his eyes. 'If you insist.'

Anisa clapped her hands together with delight when Zhanna told her to get her raincoat.

Three minutes later they were climbing into Anatoly's bombproofed Mercedes 4x4, Dawa at the wheel and her father in the passenger seat.

Zhanna looked back at the fine old colonial mansion as they drove off into the early morning; the whitewashed walls illuminated by floodlights, the elegant black timber frame bristling with security cameras.

Was it her *home*? Zhanna wasn't really sure she even knew what a home was.

There had been a dozen houses like this. Dubai, Tokyo, San Francisco, Cairo. Her father never stopped moving, travelling the world ceaselessly in the quest for the next big business deal. Zhanna had tagged along in his private jet, often feeling like excess baggage, dumped into one international school after another, making friends for a term or two then forced to say goodbye and start all over again somewhere else.

They sped out of the city, heading for the East Region where rainforest could still be found. Zhanna was watching the route finder on her smartphone, following the directions the teacher had given her and calling them out to Dawa.

Anatoly was on his mobile all the way, barking instructions to business associates in Sydney and Hong Kong, Tokyo and Manila. He barely glanced out of the window.

'Here!' Zhanna told Dawa half an hour later.

He turned off the highway on to a slender track. The trail was overgrown, spiky fronds clunked heavily against the windscreen as the vehicle bucked through the potholes. A light rain began, speckling the windows.

Zhanna felt a tremor of excitement; she loved the idea of going on a jungle trek, photographing wildlife, the tropical trees. Soon it would be daybreak and they would be able to start.

'I'm so happy,' Anisa whispered to her. 'Thank you for bringing me along.'

Zhanna squeezed her hand.

The vehicle arrived at a small clearing; the sandy red floor littered with tamarind seedpods and discarded junk.

Zhanna bit her lip when she saw the rubbish scattered about. She had wanted to feel like a jungle explorer. Litter hadn't come into that scenario.

'My teacher said we'd have to trek for half an hour to find them,' Zhanna said.

They could see a footpath disappearing into the forest.

Dawa turned off the engine. He left the sidelights on.

Raindrops drummed hard on the roof. Wet white noise. The passengers unclipped their seatbelts.

Anatoly checked his watch.

'It's still twenty minutes to daybreak,' he said, tapping his fingers against the dashboard. 'Let's have a cup of tea while we wait.'

Dawa brought out a flask and the car filled with the sharp aroma of tannin.

'Wait.' Dawa put his fingers to his lips. He pointed into the forest.

'What?' Zhanna strained to see.

'Over there,' he whispered. 'You see the eyes?'

The wipers swept in a languid pass across the screen.

'No.'

Then Zhanna saw them. Glittering pinpoints, crystal bright.

Her father stared into the darkness.

'I see one of your precious monkeys,' he said. 'There's another.'

'Oh.' Zhanna couldn't keep the disappointment out of her voice. 'They're here in the car park? I thought we'd have to go deep into the jungle to find them.'

Zhanna squinted into the forest. Rain smeared the view. The trees were dancing, every leaf alive with the rhythm of a tropical wind. Creepers swayed. Shapes swung from branch to branch with liquid grace, velvet dark, barely discernible from the night that surrounded them.

Anatoly pressed a button. His window hummed open. Just a crack. The electric buzz of night creatures punched through the saturated air.

'Come to daddy!' he called gently.

He reached into the glove box and pulled out a bag of crisps.

The hairs on the back of Zhanna's neck spiked uncomfortably as her father popped open the packet.

'I don't think we should feed them … ' she said.

Anatoly threw a handful of crisps out of the window.

'Papa!'

'Shhh!' he whispered sharply. 'Don't scare them.'

Something heavy thudded on to the bonnet. A flash of fur, the sweep of a tail. Anisa's arm jerked in surprise. A splash of scalding tea spilled on to Zhanna's thigh.

'Ow!'

Anisa dabbed a tissue on Zhanna's leg.

'I can see them getting closer,' Anatoly pulled out more crisps. 'They've smelt breakfast.'

'We shouldn't!' Zhanna cried.

Anatoly laughed, holding a crisp up to the crack.

A monkey jumped up. A leathery claw gripped the top edge of the glass.

'Hey, little one,' Anatoly said.

Restless eyes stared through the window, swimming in the distortion of the rain.

'Not much more than a baby.'

The paw came in, snatched at the crisp; pulled it out into the night. Sharp white teeth flashed. A furious squeal announced a rival had arrived.

Anatoly held up another crisp. The fingers came back in. Anatoly hit the button and the window zoomed back up.

'Got him!'

The monkey was trapped by its paw.

Zhanna gave a cry. She heard Anisa gasp.

Feet smashed against the window. The monkey screamed in terror. The paw bunched up tight, the fingers rigid.

Shapes came quickly out of the night. A snarl sent Zhanna's heart racing. The feet beat faster, the monkey twisted, looking frantically left and right.

'Let him go!' Zhanna gasped.

Anatoly laughed.

'Why stop the fun?' he said. 'You wanted to see monkeys didn't you?'

Fur flew. Drops of urine sprayed against the glass.

A shape beat against the trapped creature. The screams reached a new high.

'The others are biting it!' Anatoly laughed. 'Teaching it a lesson for being so stupid.'

Zhanna pushed against her father's hand, hit the button to bring the window down.

The monkey pulled free, and ran howling into the night.

'Law of the jungle,' Anatoly said. 'Pretty funny eh?' He went back to his phone.

Zhanna felt tears prick her eyes, then Anisa's warm hand on hers. Dawa looked back at her with a sympathetic frown.

'Let's go home,' Zhanna said. 'I don't want to do this any more.'

Zhanna's Story:
A birthday surprise

Breakfast the next morning.

'You still moping about that stupid monkey?' Anatoly regarded Zhanna over his newspaper.

Zhanna did not respond. She could not look her father in the eye. She pushed the muesli mush around the bowl.

'It was just a few bites,' he continued. 'It's probably perfectly fine.'

Zhanna crossed to the sink. The dish crashed in. Anisa placed a soothing hand on her shoulder, then quickly gathered up the broken pieces.

'You should learn to get your emotions under control,' Anatoly snapped.

Zhanna went to her room. And there she stayed, the door locked, sleeping only fitfully and refusing food for the rest of the weekend.

'You've let yourself go,' Anisa admonished her when she finally emerged. 'Your hair's all greasy. Why don't you have a nice long bath and I'll brush the knots out.'

Zhanna did as she was asked, the tangles of stress unravelling as the kindly Indonesian maid worked gently on her long hair.

'Dawa and I are making some plans for your birthday,' Anisa told her. 'But it's top secret.'

Zhanna smiled, her eyes welling up a little at the words. She was lucky to have Dawa and Anisa, she knew. Sometimes she thought, they cared for her more than her own father.

As for her real mother, all Zhanna knew was that she had died in childbirth. Apart from that brutal and disturbing fact, her father had refused to tell her more.

Zhanna's twelfth birthday came up three days later. The house filled with the aroma of baking as Anisa made the girl's favourite chocolate cake.

Zhanna wasn't surprised when her father did nothing to mark the day. There wasn't even an email.

'Never mind that,' Dawa said when she told them this bleak fact. 'We're taking you on a mystery trip.'

'You'd better bring your trekking boots and your camera,' Anisa added with a mischievous wink.

They got a nasty look from the security guard on the gate as they drove out. Excursions were supposed to be agreed by Anatoly and this one certainly hadn't been. Dawa drove them out of town, east again with the dawn, but to a different area of rainforest in a more remote spot.

'No litter on the ground here,' Anisa smiled as they parked up. 'And just listen.'

They got out and stood in silence as the sun rose over the forest canopy, breathing in the musty scent of composting leaves, relishing the curious buzzes and tweets and zitherings of birds and insects.

'Let's go!' Zhanna whispered.

They packed some water and sandwiches in their

rucksacks and entered the magical world of the rainforest.

Zhanna was sharp-eyed and observant, often spotting things that Dawa and Anisa had missed: a profusion of smoky grey caterpillars coating the bark of a magnificent old tree – thousands of them huddled together head to tail, the spiky black hairs on their backs a warning to predators.

A hummingbird hovered at the mouth of a vivid scarlet flower; seen for a second or two then gone in a feathery flash of luminescent green light.

They began to climb, the heat of the day starting to bite as they ascended a jungle ridge. A spectacular valley opened up beneath them, the canopy rippling like the surface of an ocean, a thousand shades of green stretching to the horizon.

'A wasps' nest!' Zhanna had spotted a smooth, almost plastic-looking oval object high in a branch.

'I'm not sure … ' Dawa said.

They watched for a while but no insects were buzzing about.

Then, most bizarrely, the plastic shell began to shift, a dark, moist eye emerging to scrutinise them.

'What is it?' Anisa gasped, stepping back.

For a few moments they stood dumbfounded. A second eye was revealed, blinking in the light. Then came a sharp furry snout.

'I know!' Zhanna exclaimed. 'It's a flying fox! He's hanging upside down with his wings wrapped around him.'

'Awesome!' Dawa murmured. 'Get a picture of him before he flies away.'

Zhanna framed a shot, taking it just as the flying fox stretched out leathery wings, gave an extravagant yawn and launched himself off the branch. He glided elegantly across the valley, disappearing into the foliage on the far side with a faint rustle of leaves.

'Magical!' she whispered.

Zhanna walked ahead, lost in the wonder of the place, enchanted by the whole experience and taking countless pictures as she went. When she turned to check Anisa and Dawa were following, she noticed that Dawa was handing the maid a flower. Anisa blushed, hiding the flower behind her back, causing Zhanna to smile.

She had wondered for a while if those two were romantically connected.

'You didn't see that!' Dawa laughed.

Zhanna knew that the servants were forbidden in their contracts to have anything more than a professional relationship, but she cared not a fig for her father's strict rules. Who was he to deny these gentle people happiness?

Another hour of trekking followed. The heat became

even more intense, the air thickening as it warmed. The trail petered out until they were moving through what felt like virgin forest. Zhanna loved the thought that they were treading in no man's land. It was thrilling to think that nobody had been in that exact spot before them.

Then they came across a pack of monkeys, a rare species, notoriously shy and difficult to spot.

'Banded leaf monkeys,' Zhanna whispered to the others as she pointed her lens. 'Hardly ever seen.'

The encounter was everything that Zhanna had hoped it would be. The monkeys settled down after a while, seeming to become used to the presence of the humans. Sitting on the roots of a great yellow flame tree, enveloped in the vanilla scent of the pollen, Zhanna watched as the creatures groomed and socialised, bickered and foraged for fruits.

It was the best photographic opportunity she had ever had.

'I think this will be your job when you are older,' Anisa said proudly. 'Working with wildlife.'

Zhanna nodded. It was an intoxicating thought.

The three of them returned to the house at sunset, bitten by mosquitoes, but happy with the adventure. The security guard on the gate didn't say much but he looked a bit surprised at their muddy and sweaty state.

Zhanna embraced both Dawa and Anisa as soon as they were in the house.

'You've given me the best birthday ever!' she told them.

Later Dawa showed them both pictures from Everest, the mountain that dominated his homeland and which he had climbed on two occasions. Zhanna was spellbound by the shots, her imagination fired by the extraordinary beauty of the scenes, but also by the savage power implicit within them.

'One day I will go back to mountain-guiding work,' Dawa told them. 'I miss having Everest in my life.'

Falling into bed later, Zhanna sleepily scanned through her photos, ecstatic with what she had got.

It had been, she reflected, a really wonderful day.

Zhanna's Story:
An inconvenient truth

Zhanna went to school the next morning, hoping to show some of her pictures of the trek to her classmates. But her geography teacher's very first words of the day made the young Russian girl's palms begin to sweat.

'We're going to continue our climate change studies,'

the teacher said, 'by looking at the negative effects of mining operations in the Indian Ocean.'

Zhanna chewed on her fingers. She knew her father was right at the heart of this dubious business and so did a lot of her friends. She bit her lip hard. The only reason the teacher didn't make the connection was that she was new.

'Are you feeling unwell, Zhanna?' the teacher asked. 'You can go to the sick room if you like?'

Zhanna clutched a tissue to her face.

'No. It's OK,' she replied. 'Just got a bit of a cold.'

The teacher nodded kindly, putting up a map of Asia and the Indian Ocean on the wall.

'Two monsoons have failed,' the teacher said. 'The summer rains that have happened like clockwork for thousands of years have stopped and we have to ask why? Many environmental groups believe the undersea mining activities of the Azkmine corporation from Russia are to blame.'

Zhanna blushed to her roots as the name of her father's company was mentioned. A few of the other students glanced at her.

'Azkmine is raking millions of tons of nickel off the sea-bed,' the teacher said. 'The side effect is a 2,000-mile-wide plume of methane *right across* the Indian Ocean. It is this gas cloud that has caused the monsoon to be diverted.'

Zhanna ran to her father's office as soon as she got home. She crashed in without knocking on the door.

'I had geography today,' she said breathlessly. 'And the name of your company came up.'

'Ah.' Anatoly closed the lid on his laptop.

Zhanna took a deep breath and continued.

'The teacher said it's all your fault,' she gushed. 'That your mining operations have plunged millions of people into poverty and starvation.'

'Rumours!' he snapped. 'There's no proof. Besides, if my company didn't mine there some other company would.'

Zhanna felt her cheeks flush hot.

'That's your answer? To the fact that millions of lives are threatened? That if you didn't do it someone else would?'

'You know nothing about business,' Anatoly hissed. 'Now concentrate on your studies and stop worrying about these crazy theories. I'll be having words with this geography teacher of yours.'

Zhanna simmered for the rest of the week, and then the Easter break came around. She was hoping to stay with a friend but her father had other plans.

'Pack enough things for a week away,' he said. 'I have a business trip and you're coming along.'

Zhanna frowned. Long experience had taught her just

how tedious her father's business trips could be. Often was the time he had left her stewing in a hotel room in some far-flung corner of the world while he entertained his contacts.

'Do I have to?' she moaned.

'It's Kathmandu. Nepal,' her father said. 'You might even see Everest.'

'Really?' Zhanna's eyes widened. She felt a shiver run down the back of her neck.

She ran back to her room and brought an image of Everest up on her iPad. She stared at the deadly looking fortress of rock and ice, wondering how it could be possible for any human being to dare to dream of the summit.

'Everest,' she whispered, reaching out and tracing the ridgeline with her finger.

That night she hardly slept.

Zhanna's Story:
Everest calling

Anatoly's private jet was fuelled up and ready to go at Singapore airport the next morning. Zhanna was delighted to discover that Anisa and Dawa would be accompanying them on the trip.

The flight took them over South East Asia and across the vast interior of India. Zhanna was glued to the window all the way, loving the glittering vastness of the Bay of Bengal, the rolling view of India's dusty plains as they passed beneath them, mysterious cities just visible through the sandy haze.

Then came the Himalaya, distant and enigmatic, stretching to the far points of the horizon. One peak soared above the rest.

'Everest!' Anisa was every bit as excited as Zhanna.

'We're coming in to land at Kathmandu,' the pilot announced later. 'Anyone who wants to come up for the view is more than welcome.'

Zhanna and Anisa rushed to the cockpit, smiling at each other, grateful for the privileges of being on a private jet.

The vision was an intoxicating one, but the scars of earthquake damage were still visible in the city. Some of the squares were filled with the rubble of collapsed buildings and temples. The odd delicate spire did rise up though, soaring with elegant grace from the confusion of Kathmandu's streets.

As a backdrop to the scene were the mountains, just as formidable and impressive as Zhanna had imagined.

'That's Everest dead ahead,' the captain told them. 'Hard to miss, really.'

Zhanna stared in wonder at the triple 'crown' of peaks: Everest, Lhotse and Nuptse, a banner of ice crystals pluming from their summit ridges. She wanted the moment to be preserved forever in her mind. Then she remembered her camera, taking a shot with the telephoto lens.

'Can't we fly closer?' she asked.

The pilot laughed. 'Sorry, we're on final approach. You need to take your seats.'

Ten minutes later they were on the ground. The aircraft was parked up in a discreet part of the airport.

Anatoly had friends in this corner of the world. A delegation of Nepali businessmen ushered them through the airport without so much as a passport check.

'Why are there so many soldiers around?' Zhanna asked.

'Better not to ask,' Dawa said. His face was glum.

'Aren't you happy to be back?' Zhanna asked him.

'This is not a good time for my country,' he replied.

Zhanna could tell he didn't want to say more.

Mercedes limousines whisked them through the congested traffic of Kathmandu, barging rickshaws and motorbikes and wandering cattle out of the way in a series of arrogant manoeuvres that had Zhanna clutching the edge of her seat.

'Slow down, please!' she cried. The driver took no notice.

A boy with a begging bowl had to leap for his life as the convoy raced past.

'Many people without a home,' Anisa whispered.

Zhanna nodded. She had seen poverty on her travels with her father but never so many people camping out in the alleyways and pavements of a city.

At one crossroads they were forced to slow. Next to them were hundreds of people in a food hand-out line, many with bare feet and some dressed in little more than rags.

'Some of them are just children,' Zhanna said. 'Where are their parents?'

'Many have died,' Dawa muttered. 'The famine has hit hard.'

'It's a natural cycle,' Anatoly snapped. 'These countries have always had periods of plenty and periods of drought.'

Dawa and Zhanna exchanged a look.

They arrived at a glitzy hotel, a five-star monument to bad taste, gilded with mirrors and bling. Sharply dressed porters rushed to open the limousine doors, ushering them into a foyer which was a palace of polished marble and tinkling fountains.

Zhanna thought about the dried-up wells out in the countryside, the crops withering from drought.

Anatoly had booked the biggest suite in the hotel. Zhanna felt ill when she opened a fridge and saw it was filled with exotic cheeses, meats and champagne. She asked the butler to remove the lavish bowls of fruit; it all felt so wrong when people were struggling with malnutrition or worse just a stone's throw across the street.

Plans were made at breakfast the next morning. Zhanna and Anisa would be free to tour the city markets and temples while Anatoly attended business meetings connected with an oil-drilling operation he was hoping to set up in Nepal.

'I'd rather go to the mountains,' Zhanna told her father. 'See Everest close up.'

'Too dangerous,' Anatoly replied. 'I've heard rumours about bandits in the highlands.'

As they left the dining room a voice suddenly called out.

'Anatoly Kuzkin? Mr Kuzkin?'

An earnest-looking young Indian man with a beard approached their party. Anatoly's face looked like thunder.

'It is you, isn't it?' the man said. 'I'm Sunjay Chopra from the *Delhi Times*. What brings you to Nepal, Mr Kuzkin? Would you be kind enough to give me a quote? Perhaps a short interview?'

'No comment.'

Anatoly ran for the lift, pulling Zhanna after him. The journalist wasn't giving up, however, and he squeezed himself into the lift beside them as the doors were closing.

'Are you here to apologise, Mr Kuzkin?' the journalist asked. He brought out a smartphone and turned on the mic as he pushed it towards Anatoly's face. 'Perhaps you have decided to donate some of your billions to the people of Nepal? It seems the least you can do after your company has destroyed the country.'

'Leave us alone!' Anatoly hissed. He pushed the phone away.

The journalist was ejected from the lift at the next floor but the incident had put Anatoly in a cranky mood.

The next day it further worsened when his assistant produced an iPad and showed him the diary piece the Indian reporter had written.

ECO-VANDAL ANATOLY KUZKIN JETS IN TO KATHMANDU

The man once named and shamed as the boss of the world's most polluting company is on a secret business trip to Nepal. This alarming news will come as a shock to the Nepali people; far from attempting to make amends for the misery his industries have inflicted since the monsoon has failed, Kuzkin is instead seeking to wreak even more havoc. Sources have revealed he is negotiating to buy up cheap land destroyed by drought and planning to drill for oil.
Is there no end to his greed?

The article ended by mentioning the name of the hotel.

'Sir, I think you should see this,' Dawa said.

Zhanna joined her father by the window of the suite.

The street outside the hotel was filled with an angry mob. There were already hundreds out there, with more flooding in with every passing moment. Some had placards bearing slogans, the paint still wet.

Zhanna flinched as a stone rattled against the window. A feathery crack splintered the glass.

There was a knock on the door. The hotel manager came in.

'Don't worry. We're packing our things,' Anatoly told him. 'We're getting out of here as fast as we can.'

'I'm not so sure, sir … ' the manager said. He took out a handkerchief, wiping sweat from his brow. 'Come and take a look out the back.'

Zhanna's Story:
The protest begins

Zhanna gasped as she saw the crowd climbing over the wall, flooding in to the hotel garden. Word that Kuzkin was in town seemed to have spread like wildfire.

'They've sealed the hotel up,' the manager said. 'No one's going anywhere. I've got our security men guarding the doors.'

'Where are the police?' Anatoly asked. 'Why aren't they doing something?'

The manager reddened. 'I don't know, sir.'

Zhanna reached a quick conclusion: the police wouldn't be showing up – they agreed with the mob. They were as angry with Anatoly as the people were.

'They'll get bored in a while,' Anatoly predicted. 'They'll disperse as soon as it gets dark.'

But the crowd did not disperse. At sunset they lit small fires. The numbers continued to swell; students, farmers, off-duty soldiers. The chanting got louder, more aggressive. There were calls for Kuzkin to come out and answer questions.

Inside the luxury suite they could hear every yell.

'What if they storm the building?' Anisa whispered to Zhanna. The crowd had not attempted to enter the hotel as yet but the situation felt perilously insecure.

'I don't know,' Zhanna replied. The thought of the mob rampaging through the corridors was a truly terrifying one.

Anatoly grabbed his mobile, trying to get hold of the Russian ambassador to Nepal. But the embassy had been closed down for weeks.

'Maybe we could get a helicopter to come in and pick us up from the roof?' Dawa suggested.

The manager soon pointed out the flaw in that plan: radio masts on the top of the building meant there was nowhere for a helicopter to land.

Zhanna found it impossible to sleep, passing long hours playing chess with Anisa and Dawa. The only release she could get from the massed anger of the people was listening to music with her headphones on, but somehow even that did not block out the cries from outside.

Looking at the pictures of the jungle trek cheered her up a little, but even that was spoiled when Anatoly came in and caught sight of the screen of her laptop.

'What are those?' he demanded.

'Ah … ' For a brief moment Zhanna was tempted to lie, tell him the shots were from a school trip. But her conscience wouldn't let her. 'Dawa and Anisa took me to see the wildlife,' she told him.

Anatoly's eyebrows twitched.

'Without my permission?'

'Yes, but it was my fault,' Zhanna said quickly. 'I was … '

'They will be punished for this,' Anatoly hissed.

The door slammed as he left the room.

The crowd did thin out a bit in the darkest hours of that first night, but plenty of the protestors seemed happy to pitch up their canvas shelters and sleep there.

An impromptu shanty town was growing up. About a thousand people were squatting in the grounds of the hotel.

At daybreak, the manager negotiated with the leaders of the crowd. The other hotel guests were permitted to leave, but not Kuzkin's group. Journalists from foreign countries began to ring the room, looking for interviews with Anatoly. The stand-off was beginning to make the news all over the world.

Anatoly came up with a new strategy – trying to find a local security company who would send armed men in to protect them. His efforts came to nothing; the people of Nepal seemed to have united against him and no one wanted to help, even when money was on the table.

During the afternoon Zhanna and Anatoly were looking down on the crowd when they saw a minibus pull up. Five foreigners climbed out and Zhanna heard her father give a sharp intake of breath.

'What's wrong?' Zhanna asked.

Anatoly pressed against the window, his eyes widening.

A woman had climbed out of the vehicle, a figure that stood out head and shoulders above the crowd. Dressed in combat gear, her platinum-blonde hair marked her out in the crowd of dark-haired Nepali protestors.

The new arrivals pulled rucksacks out of the minibus. Zhanna could see the distinctive white tags of airline baggage labels on the handles. It looked like they had just flown in to Kathmandu. The tall woman appeared to be in charge of the group; she definitely seemed to be bossing the others around.

They began to erect some tents.

'Who is she?' Zhanna asked.

The woman looked up, her eyes seeming to lock directly on to Anatoly. Zhanna shrunk back into the shadows. Slowly, the woman raised her hand in a pistol shape, aiming at Anatoly, miming a shot, and then blowing on her fingers with a thin smile.

'She ... ' Anatoly seemed about to say something. Then his expression changed and he clamped his mouth shut.

'What?' Zhanna asked. 'Do you know her?'

Anatoly abruptly drew the curtains.

'Go to your bedroom,' he said, 'and don't come out until I tell you to.'

Zhanna did as she was told, sheer exhaustion enabling her to snatch some restless, unconscious hours.

In her darkened dreams the blonde-haired woman had a starring role. Tormentor. Interrogator. Leader of the pack.

Who is she? Zhanna wondered. *Why had she come? And why had her father reacted the way he did?*

Zhanna's Story:
Traitors and trauma

The siege entered the third day. The tall blonde woman was still there and the crowd was as vocal as ever. A pile of car tyres had been set alight, sending a noxious cloud of thick black smoke towards the hotel. The smell of burning rubber made Zhanna feel sick.

Anatoly was red-eyed from lack of sleep. His efforts to enlist help had drawn a frustrating blank.

'My "friends" seem to be reluctant to get involved,' he bemoaned.

The manager came up to see them several times a day, but his visits only soured Anatoly's mood even further.

A local newspaper had printed a photograph of the interior of the suite on the second day and Anatoly got it into his head that one of the hotel staff must have sold it to the paper.

'Your people can't be trusted,' he told the manager.

An impromptu kitchen had opened up in the corner of the hotel garden. The presence of free curry and rice was drawing in a seemingly endless stream of protestors.

Dawa was spending long periods of time on his mobile, a habit that seemed to provoke Anatoly.

'Who the hell are you talking to?' he barked. 'Is it you that's talking to the press? Sending photos to them?'

'No, sir,' Dawa replied. 'I'm talking to my cousin.'

'Why? Can he help us?'

'Maybe, sir. He's out there in the crowd.'

The room fell quiet. Anatoly went rigid. Zhanna saw the veins stand out at his temple.

She realised straight away that Dawa had made a big mistake.

'Your cousin is out there?' Anatoly repeated.

Dawa blushed deep red. A thin sheen of perspiration broke out on his brow.

'Yes, sir.'

'And you are in contact with him?'

Dawa nodded his head, licking his lips nervously, his eyes flicking rapidly from Zhanna to Anatoly.

'So, you are a traitor,' Anatoly continued, his tone menacingly quiet. 'Colluding with the enemy, giving them information?'

'No, sir … ' Dawa blustered. 'I thought if we got a dialogue going with some of the protestors, maybe we could … '

'Anisa! Get in here now!'

The servant hurried in, white in the face, her normally calm expression creased with worry lines.

'Have you taken Zhanna on an excursion without my permission?'

Anisa gasped.

'Also, what is your relationship with Dawa?'

'Sir, if I could just … ' Dawa began.

'I've seen the two of you holding hands on the security cameras back in Singapore,' Anatoly continued. 'Such a relationship is forbidden under the terms of your contract. And in the light of what I now know about Dawa, that makes you both a liability.'

'Sir, I promise … ' Anisa stammered.

'You are both fired,' he said.

'No!' Zhanna put her arm around Anisa's shoulder.

The maid was trembling with shock.

'Dawa, you can pack your things right away and take your chances with the crowd outside. No doubt your cousin will welcome you with open arms. Anisa, you will fly back with us to Singapore when we get out of this mess and I'll arrange your return to Indonesia.'

'But Papa, you can't … ' Zhanna began.

'There's no discussion,' Anatoly said firmly. 'My decision is final. You're both fired.'

Zhanna pleaded. She begged. And the more agitated she became the more her father stonewalled the situation. Finally she threw a glass of milk at the wall, shattering it into shards as her father looked on in disgust.

'The more you protest the more determined I become,' he shrugged.

Dawa and Anisa were fired from his team and that was that.

Zhanna asked to talk to Dawa before he left but her father forbade it. The gentle Nepali wasn't even allowed to say farewell to Anisa.

'You're a stupid little girl,' Anatoly raged at Zhanna. 'There are plenty more servants out there who will do a better job. Those two have disobeyed my rules and they are now paying the price.'

'They took me to the jungle,' Zhanna told him, defiantly. 'Took me on a birthday treat which was the best day of my life. Better than any day you ever gave me.'

'Even more reason,' Anatoly snorted, 'to get rid of them.'

Zhanna's Story:
Breaking free

Zhanna hurried to her room, burying her head beneath the duvet of her bed until Anisa came in.

'Has Dawa gone?' Zhanna asked her.

'Yes.' Anisa's eyes were, like Zhanna's, puffy and raw. 'He made it through the crowd without any problems, but I'm not sure if I will ever see him again.'

Anisa's fingers clutched tightly at Zhanna's hand.

'But you must have an email address for him?' Zhanna asked. 'A mobile number or something?'

Anisa sighed. A single glistening tear ran down her cheek.

'Your father confiscated his phone. I've got no other contact for him. I remember the name of his village but nothing else … '

'This is all so unfair.' Zhanna sprang to her feet, pacing the room. 'I hate my stupid father! Really, I hate him!'

'Don't,' Anisa said. She placed a trembling hand on Zhanna's arm. 'There's nothing we can do now. I just have to accept my fate. But losing Dawa will be hard. He had even mentioned marriage.'

Zhanna gave Anisa a great big hug.

'You don't have to lose him,' she said.

'What do you mean?'

'Why don't you follow him?' Zhanna proposed. 'You've been sacked after all. You're free to go, aren't you?'

Anisa laughed at the audacity of the proposal, then her face clouded.

'I can't do that,' she said. 'How would I find him? Where would I go?'

'You know the name of his village, yes?'

'Lukla, near Everest,' Anisa nodded.

'So? All you have to do is get yourself there.'

For a moment Anisa stared at Zhanna, as if the idea was taking root. But then she shook her head.

'You've been watching too many movies,' she said sadly. 'I don't have the courage to do that.'

She gave Zhanna a kiss goodnight and slipped silently from the room.

Zhanna felt sick to her stomach that night. The sound of the protestors cut endlessly through the walls of the bedroom. Someone had brought some drums into the crowd and the rhythm of their beat went on for hours as Zhanna tried and failed to sleep.

The army took action at dawn on the fourth day of the protest. Anatoly had bribed a high-ranking officer to clear the crowd outside the hotel.

The first thing Zhanna knew about it was the squeal of brakes as the jeeps pulled up. A megaphone barked into life, instructions yelled in a guttural tone. The clamour of cries increased abruptly in volume. She rushed to the window with Anisa, watching in horror as the military men tore down the temporary shelters and began to burn them.

The crowd panicked. Opposition was brutally suppressed. Gunstocks and batons flew as the protestors were beaten.

To Zhanna's surprise, the blonde woman and her friends did not fight back. They shouldered their rucksacks and melted into the alleyways on the other side of the road.

'The foreigners have given up,' Anisa said.

'Yes,' Zhanna replied, uneasily. It seemed strange to her that the ferocious-looking warrior woman had slunk away without a fight.

A water cannon opened up, drenching the protestors and

extinguishing the braziers they had been huddled around for warmth overnight. The jet dampened the spirit of the crowd and soon they were dispersing in all directions with the army in hot pursuit.

'Good result!' Anatoly was jubilant. 'Let's get to the airport.'

A minibus was quickly brought to the front of the hotel. Anisa clutched Zhanna's hand tighter than ever as the vehicle pulled away into the streets with an army escort front and rear.

'We'll be out of here in the next couple of hours,' Anatoly said. 'It's a shame because there are good profits to be made in Nepal if only it were a calmer place.'

'Profits?' Zhanna blurted out. 'That's all you think about! That's why the people are against you … '

At the airport they were held in a waiting area. After a delay of an hour, the airport manager arrived with unwelcome news.

'Your aeroplane has been vandalised,' the group was told. 'A mob broke through the perimeter wall and damaged the undercarriage and wing.'

A series of frantic telephone calls followed. Spare parts and a technician would have to be flown from Switzerland. Six days was the minimum estimate to get the private jet back in the air.

Anatoly decided to stay in Nepal and explore the business options for a dam in the far east of the country, a remote zone where he would not be recognised.

'You can fly out to Singapore with SilkAir tomorrow morning,' he told Zhanna. 'Anisa can keep you company before she goes back to Indonesia.'

Zhanna felt the heaviness in her heart lift as she watched Anatoly and two business associates fly out in a helicopter later that afternoon. Her world always felt so much lighter without her father around.

Zhanna and Anisa were checked in to an airport hotel where they both ordered burger and chips from room service.

They ate in silence, locked in their own thoughts until Anisa turned on the TV. The news was running and the lead report was from a town on the trail to Everest Base Camp.

'Did he say Lukla?' Zhanna said, in surprise. 'Wasn't that the town that Dawa comes from?'

Anisa leaned closer to the screen. 'Yes … ' she frowned.

The images showed youths running in a muddy alleyway. Soldiers were following them, firing smoking canisters of tear gas.

'They're fighting in the mountains,' Anisa said. 'Some sort of rebellion?'

Anisa sat beside the young Russian girl as images of rioting filled the screen.

'This is the last thing I need to see right now,' Anisa said.

A reporter was ducking for cover in the midst of the protest. Stones and banners were whizzing just over his head as soldiers pushed against the crowd.

'Dawa is somewhere there,' Anisa added miserably.

The video images cut to a different part of the town, an open area outside a big lodge. The camera locked on to a young woman with a baby. Somehow she had become swept up in the chaos. Tear gas was swirling through the air. The woman was clutching her baby to her chest as she struggled to try and stay on her feet.

Soldiers ran at the protestors. A policeman was screaming something at the camera. Fists and wooden staves were flying left and right. The woman fell under the blows. A passer-by rushed through the shot.

Anisa suddenly went stiff.

'That was Dawa!' she cried. 'I saw him!'

'Where?'

Zhanna craned forward. The camera jerked left, then right, the image a blur as the camera operator was jostled.

'Are you sure?'

'I … I think so.'

The camera snapped into focus once more.

'Yes! There he is again!' Zhanna cried.

A figure seemed to be trying to shield the woman as the crowd panicked. Dozens of protestors fell to the ground. The man was lost beneath them. The view was fleeting, little more than a shadow seen side on. But it really had looked like Dawa.

Soldiers lunged into the crowd.

The scene cut again. Back to the studio where the news announcer moved smoothly on to a different story.

Anisa and Zhanna stared at each other in silence for a few seconds.

'Do you think he was hurt?' Anisa said. 'It looked like the soldiers were hitting him.'

'He's tough,' Zhanna replied. 'With a bit of luck he … '

Anisa went to the window, staring out of the shutters at the airport terminal building. 'This has changed my mind,' she said quietly. 'I'm going to the mountains to find him.'

Zhanna clapped her hands.

'I'll pay for it.'

Anisa's eyes widened.

'But … you don't have to. It's my problem not yours … '

Zhanna put a finger to Anisa's lips.

'It's a gift from me. I mean it.'

Anisa smiled uncertainly. Then a shadow passed across her brow.

'I've never been anywhere on my own before.'

Zhanna stared at her for a few moments. Then her face lit up.

'I'll go with you,' she said, simply. 'Why not?'

Anisa's mouth fell open. 'Seriously?'

'We can delay the flight back to Singapore by a couple of days,' Zhanna proposed. 'Papa will be in the mountains in the east for a week anyway so chances are he won't even notice. Besides, he rarely pays much attention to where I am and what I'm doing.'

Fixing a flight to Lukla was a simple matter the next morning. The local routes were cheap and quick to book.

Zhanna smiled as the helicopter prepared to take off. She clutched tightly on to Anisa's hand.

'We'll find Dawa,' Anisa said. 'I'm sure of it. Even if we have to go to Everest, we'll find him.'

Everest. Zhanna felt her stomach perform a loop the loop as the aircraft rose shakily into the turbulent sky.

They would soon be in the presence of the mightiest mountain on earth.

CHAPTER 7

It was 4 a.m. when Zhanna's whispered story came to a close. Swaddled in our cosy little den inside the supply tent, Tashi and I had listened in rapt attention through the deadest, coldest hours of the night.

Dawn would creep up on us in the next hour or so. It was time to think about getting back to Kami and the others.

Tashi and I made sure Zhanna was safe and secure in her hiding place. Then we slunk out on to the frigid glacier, taking a circuitous route back to the tent where Kami and the others would, no doubt, be wondering where we were.

'Oh no!' Tashi murmured. The guards were still there, huddled together outside our tent.

We hunkered down in a hollow about thirty metres away,

shivering and praying the men would shift. The tiny sliver of moon was just falling behind the bulk of Everest, plunging the glacier into total darkness.

One of the bosses came out to check the guards just before 5 a.m. We were close enough to hear the two half-frozen men pleading for a break. Finally the man agreed they could come and grab a tea to warm up.

'They're all asleep in there anyway,' he said.

The guards left and we sneaked back into the tent, frozen to the marrow, just twenty minutes before dawn.

'Way to go!' Alex whispered, clapping us on the back as Dawa took the gun. The others were also awake and had been waiting anxiously for our return.

'We found Zhanna,' Tashi told them.

'Wonderful!' Kami's face glowed with pleasure at the news.

We told the story of Zhanna's hiding place, breaking off abruptly when one of our captors grudgingly brought in hot water. Shreeya made tea and handed each of us a weak cupful.

'Terrible for her,' Alex said. 'Not knowing from one moment to the next if she'll be discovered.'

'Awful – so lonely,' Shreeya agreed. 'We have to get her to safety somehow.'

Tashi and I distributed the blankets we had brought back

and then curled up in the corner of the tent to get a couple of hours' rest after our sleepless night.

We awoke late morning, and for the rest of the day time crawled by in a curious kind of nervous tension.

Visits to the nearby toilet tent were allowed, an armed guard standing by at all times.

Food was delivered. Canned tuna, crackers and chocolate. We shared it out carefully so that each of us got a fair portion. I couldn't stomach the tuna but I did manage to force down some crackers. They gave us cold water to drink.

Tashi reached for my hand. I put my arm around her, hugging her tight. It was good to feel her so close.

As another night fell, Kami and Shreeya whispered comforting words to one another. We all felt the extra pressure that Shreeya's pregnancy brought to the situation. It wasn't just Shreeya's life at stake. There was the baby to think about.

That second night was bitterly cold and seemingly endless. Without any head torches we were plunged into darkness as soon as the sun set. We had some sleeping bags but no mats. Lying directly on the ice of the glacier, we were tossing and shivering for hours until we huddled together for warmth. Even then we got little rest.

The cracks and creaks of the restless ice seemed even spookier than ever.

'She wants us weakened,' Alex surmised. 'Less of a handful if we're exhausted.'

'Clever, except for one thing,' Shreeya pointed out. 'Her guards are suffering even more.'

One of them, the guy with blue lips, was showing stronger signs of altitude sickness. He disappeared behind a boulder from time to time and we heard the distinctive sound of retching.

'He won't be able to take much more,' Alex said.

I kept thinking about poor Zhanna, trapped in her hiding place.

Viking came out several times to check her men were keeping a good watch. She swore at them when she saw they were dozing on the job. The men snapped to attention. They were obviously terrified of her.

Kami was shivering even more than the rest of us. His years of paralysis seemed to have left him more vulnerable to the cold.

Just after dawn, Viking strode out again. Her face was fixed with a determined expression as she switched on her megaphone. 'Zhanna! I know you're out there. I can feel it.'

She waited. No reply came back.

'My men are watching the trails to the south,' she continued. 'We know you must still be in the camp, hungry, thirsty, cold. You can't last much longer, you must know that.'

The world went still. The only noise was the cawing of rooks on the rubbish heaps and the thundering of our hearts.

'We should start to kill the hostages,' one of Viking's men muttered.

Shreeya put her head in her hands.

'I can't bear it,' she sobbed.

Shreeya doubled up and retched into the corner of the tent. Tashi gripped me hard on the arm.

'You're forgetting our agreement,' Viking hissed to the man. He spat on the ground and walked away, shoulders hunched.

The megaphone squawked again.

'Your friends are going to pay a price, Zhanna. I'm going to remove all their blankets and sleeping bags. They will get no food from now on until you give yourself up.'

That morning was terrible.

Viking had been true to her word. Every scrap of warm bedding was snatched away from us and we were given no food or liquid of any sort. We had hidden the gun beneath a rock in the corner of the tent and it was not found. That was one positive.

'She's going crazy,' Tashi said. We were huddled together, like emperor penguins, sharing our body heat.

'Her men are getting more aggressive,' I added. 'The danger is if she loses control of the whole situation.'

'We will die if this continues,' Dawa muttered. 'We have to try and escape.'

'I agree,' Alex said. 'Escape is our only option.'

'We could rush the guards,' Dawa proposed. 'Get enough weapons to shoot our way out. How many of you know how to handle a gun?'

No one replied.

'You're the only one who has those skills,' Alex said. 'Besides, they must figure we might try a stunt like that. Better we think of something they're not expecting.'

'Priority number one has to be getting Shreeya out,' Tashi said. 'Every extra day she spends up here could put the baby at risk.'

'The guards are getting more and more exhausted,' Dawa said. 'And we already know how badly acclimatised they are.'

'We need a distraction,' Alex said. 'Something to draw

them away.'

Shreeya was sick again that afternoon. Her condition seemed to be worsening. She sat in miserable silence, clutching her belly.

'I'm really worried about her,' Kami confided in one of our whispered conversations. 'At the very least we have to negotiate with Viking to get the girls out of here.'

'Negotiate?' Alex retorted. 'She's never going to listen to reason.'

The conversation went on for hours. Crazy ideas were discussed and dismissed. Night began to fall. Day three of the siege was coming to an end and we still had no plan to get out.

Then Alex's eyes brightened.

'How about the fuel tent?' he said. 'The one with all the butane cylinders? Maybe a couple of us can sneak out and set them alight. Draw the terrorists away so that everyone else can escape?'

Kami nodded.

'An explosion!' he exclaimed. 'Viking and her men will have to try and save the cylinders. They can't survive for long up here without gas.'

Dawa nodded. 'I like the plan,' he said. 'It's the best idea we've had. Plus I've got the gun here in case we get any opposition to the escape part of things ... '

I saw Tashi reach out for Shreeya's hand.

'Girls? Do you agree with the plan?' Alex asked.

Tashi and Shreeya thought for a few seconds.

'I agree,' Shreeya said slowly. 'But we have to take Zhanna with us, OK?'

'Definitely,' Tashi agreed. 'No escape plan unless Zhanna comes with us.'

We talked about the logistics of rescuing Zhanna, and then a thought came to me.

'Hang on a minute,' I said to Alex. 'How are you going to set that tent on fire? I mean without blowing yourself up at the same time?'

'Put one of the butane cylinders next to a naked flame,' he replied, 'and open the valve.'

'Would that give you time to get away?'

'I guess ... then we'll follow you guys down the glacier.'

'And the naked flame?' Kami questioned.

'A candle,' Dawa suggested. 'Anyone got one?'

An urgent search of the tent began. We found a stub of a candle and a cigarette lighter in the storage trunk in the corner.

'You can't do this alone,' Kami said to Alex. 'And Dawa has to be here because he's the only one who can handle a gun. So either Ryan or I must go with you.'

There was a long silence. My eyes flickered to Tashi. Leaving her to try and escape without me went against every instinct.

'Maybe we should draw straws,' Kami said.

We all agreed. It was the only fair way.

Alex tore two strips off a piece of scrap paper, turning his back on us to place them in his closed fist. Kami and I took turns, my heart sinking as I pulled the shortest one.

Tashi looked away. I could see she was gutted.

We continued talking long into the night. The guards were on their last legs now, hardly able to stand.

'Viking's resting in her tent while her men are freezing half to death,' Alex observed. 'They're starting to complain about her.'

One of the guards became sick. He vomited a few times and even came into the tent to ask us for medicine.

'This is perfect for us,' Alex said. 'They're falling like flies. We'll go for it tonight.'

At 10 p.m. I tried to rest. Sleep remained tantalisingly out of reach. Alex's plan was reckless and brilliant all at once.

It could so easily end in disaster. But the counter strategy – remaining as hostages – was equally lethal. Viking's men were becoming unpredictable and ever-more desperate.

We had to take the initiative and get out of this mess as fast as we could.

I fell into a kind of half sleep. At 2 a.m. we heard the distant sound of a helicopter engine.

'Rescue?' Alex whispered. The guards hardly stirred. The engine noise soon faded away and I dozed again.

At 3 a.m. Alex shook me awake.

'All the guards are asleep,' he whispered. 'Let's go and set the world on fire.'

We woke the others, telling them to stand by and make a break for it as soon as the fire kicked off.

Dawa retrieved the gun from its hiding place.

'Good luck,' Tashi whispered. I held her tight. Kami and Shreeya embraced me.

I gently eased up the canvas and Alex and I made fast progress away from the tent. Then we heard an unwelcome sound.

Footsteps.

'Stay still!' Alex breathed.

A guard was on the move. Heading in our direction. As the footsteps crunched towards us, we pressed ourselves tight to the ice, trying to merge with the dark shadows of the rocks. My heart went into overdrive.

The guard stopped. Took a pee. Then he returned to the front of the tent.

We waited a few minutes then went on, trying not to break through the ice on the frozen puddles.

'So far so good,' Alex whispered.

After a few hundred metres of progress we entered a natural bottleneck in the glacier. A place where the terrain became so dissected with faults and collapsed holes that we were forced on to a path.

We sped up, hoping to get past as quickly as possible. The main terrorist tent was fifty metres to our right.

A bitter argument seemed to be raging inside. A woman's voice was dominant.

'Viking,' Alex murmured. 'Does she ever sleep?'

We continued, reaching our destination after twenty minutes of hard slog. The butane tent was easy to spot. It was one of the few white tents at Base Camp. Certainly the only one with a massive Hazchem symbol emblazoned on its side.

We sneaked right up.

There was no guard in sight.

'We're on!' Alex whispered, gripping my arm.

We moved stealthily across the ice, then pressed ourselves

into the darkness at the back of the tent, listening for the sound of voices or snores coming from within.

Nothing.

We entered the tent. The butane cylinders were stacked in a neat pile.

'We're in business.' I could see the gleam of excitement in Alex's eyes.

Working as quietly as we could, we rearranged things, placing one of the gas cylinders in the middle of the others, effectively building a tower around it.

'OK? Everything ready?'

I flicked the cigarette lighter into life. The candle flared up.

Alex twisted the top of the gas cylinder. The stench of butane quickly began to fill the tent. We kept low as we left, using the natural cover of the undulating dips and hollows of the glacier.

We found some rocks to hide behind. A minute passed. Then another.

'Something's wrong,' I whispered to Alex. 'It's taking forever.'

'Maybe the candle went out?' he replied.

And then the explosion split the night air. A fireball tens of metres across flared into the sky.

'Yes!' Alex hissed.

Screams rang out. The terrorists ran out of their command tent. Viking was one of the first.

The gas store went up in a blast of sparks and flames. Then came a much bigger detonation as one of the cylinders exploded.

We saw Viking, her distinctive silhouette backlit by the fire, running to and fro, trying to gather some of her men together.

'Rescue some of the bottles,' she screamed. Two of her men tried to get into the tent but were beaten back by the heat.

It was mayhem. Exactly what we wanted.

Perfect circumstances for the others to escape.

More of Viking's men began to emerge from the darkness. We recognised two of the guards who had been watching our tent.

Now it was time for us to sneak away, work our way back through the night, following our friends and hopefully catching them up before daybreak.

'Let's go!' Alex said.

We hurried south, down the glacier. Behind us, more of the terrorists were flocking to the burning gas store.

Then, ahead of us, came a shot. And another.

Had something gone wrong with the escape? Were those shots from Dawa? Or from one of the terrorists?

I tried to calm my mind but it was hard not to imagine the worst. My heart raced out of control.

Tashi. Was she OK? I would never forgive myself for not being with her if something had gone wrong.

Fifteen minutes later we saw two shadowy figures coming fast towards us.

Alex hissed a warning. I ducked down. Then I realised it was Dawa and Kami, both struggling for breath.

'What's happened?' I asked, my gut churning with a dread sensation. 'Where are the girls?'

'The whole thing got messed up,' Kami gasped. 'One of the guards stayed behind when the explosion kicked off. He spotted us and pulled a gun.'

'I sorted him out,' Dawa added. 'But then others came. It was total chaos and we got separated from the girls.'

'Oh no!'

'There are still some guards following us,' Kami whispered, glancing over his shoulder into the darkness of the glacier.

'Do you think the girls got away?' I demanded.

'We think so, yes,' Kami replied hesitantly. 'But it was

mayhem down there so we can't be sure.'

We heard the clatter of boots in the distance, a sharp command in a foreign tongue.

'We have to keep moving,' Alex said.

A torch beam swept in our direction.

'There they are!' called a voice.

We turned, hurrying in the only direction we could: north towards the end of the valley. Away from the girls. Ahead of us was the deadly maze of the Icefall.

Could we hide in there? I wondered. *Would Kami remember it from his last expedition and find us a safe refuge? Or would we be trapped? Picked off by Viking's gunmen.*

Our situation was quickly spiralling out of control.

We puffed and panted across the rocky surface of the glacier.

'One more thing,' Kami said breathlessly. 'We couldn't find Zhanna. She wasn't in the tent.'

'Then where on earth is she?' Alex replied.

'I have no idea. She must have decided to make a break down the glacier.'

A shout cut through the night air. It was Viking's voice. It seemed she had abandoned the burning gas store and was now concentrating on hunting us down. There was no breath left to debate Zhanna's mysterious disappearance.

We could only keep moving, lungs struggling for air.

Next time we looked back we realised there were even more pursuers. At least a dozen head torches bobbed in the darkness.

Our beautiful plan, I thought, *turned to pure chaos*.

A shriek rang out. Viking calling for more men.

We rushed onwards, passing the wreckage of some ransacked tents, jumping the small river of meltwater that ran on the eastern edge of the glacier.

The first streaks of dawn were chasing away the night.

'This way!' Kami said.

He led us into the lower section of the Icefall, navigating on instinct. We were slipping on the ice, no crampon spikes on our boots. Shots rang out behind us once again.

I ducked, my spine tingling.

'I've got an idea,' Kami blurted out. 'Let's cross one of the crevasses and pull over the ladder so they can't follow.'

I scanned the terrain; saw a huge crevasse just ahead.

We had a slender chance of survival. The tiniest glimmer of hope ignited inside me.

A ladder spanned it. Kami was right: all we had to do was pull that ladder over and we would be safe. At least for a while.

A sudden cry came from our right. Two of Viking's men

were standing just fifty metres away – guards positioned at the top end of the camp.

'Get down!' Dawa hissed.

One of the men pulled out a gun. We dived for cover.

Spurts of ice kicked up beside us as he fired. My heart pounded fit to burst. Another shot split the air.

Alex's body jerked backwards. He gasped in surprise.

He fell with a thud. His body twitched, his eyes didn't seem to be able to focus.

'No!' Kami's scream cut through the air.

We pulled Alex behind a wall of ice. I snatched a quick look over the top. A spume of crystals erupted next to my face.

Alex clutched at my arm. Blood ran from his mouth.

'What can we do?' Kami cried.

I risked another look. Viking and her thugs were now shockingly close to our position. Weaving through the lower parts of the Icefall. Coming fast.

Dawa pulled out his pistol.

'I'll hold them off,' the Nepali said. 'Buy you some time.'

He moved swiftly. The sound of two rapid shots ripped up the air.

We turned to Alex, pulling his Gore-Tex jacket aside.

'Alex!' Kami said. 'Hang on in there.'

For a few seconds it seemed he recognised us. The light of understanding in his eyes. Then he moaned, a deep and terrible call of pain.

'Stay with us!' I cried. 'Stay with us, Alex.'

Alex was slipping in and out of consciousness, his shirt already soaked with dark red blood.

The terrible sound of air sucking from the hole in his chest told us the worst. I ripped open his shirt.

In his chest was a ragged hole. The bullet wound was right next to his heart.

Then his eyes opened again, refocused.

'Kami,' he said slowly. 'Are we cool?'

The slick, liquid crystal of a single tear trickled down Kami's cheek. He eased the pressure on Alex's neck, where his friend's jacket had twisted awkwardly.

Dawa rattled off another two shots. Rifle blasts came in return, the air filling with ice chips as the sérac took the hits.

'We're cool, Alex. We're more than cool,' Kami said.

'That's good,' he said. 'I'm happy about that.'

Kami rolled up Alex's jacket and placed it tenderly behind his head.

'I've stalled them,' Dawa called. 'I think I hit two but not Viking.'

'Let me see the mountain,' Alex whispered.

We propped him up so he could look to the north. The bulk of Everest was hidden behind a nearby ridgeline, but the summit was standing proud above it, peerless and above all else on earth.

'There she is,' Alex whispered. 'My muse, inspiration, nemesis.'

The tip of Everest was suddenly flooded with golden light from the rising sun. The clouds above it seemed a crown of deepest violet.

Alex reached for Kami's hand. He held it tight.

'One day you'll make it, Kami,' he said. 'One day the shrine bell will help you get to the top.'

A tremor ran through him. Flecks of blood appeared at his lips.

'I believe so,' Kami said. 'I truly do.'

'And you too Ryan,' he said to me. 'Say a prayer for me on top?'

'For sure,' I replied, somehow forcing the words out.

Alex Brennan shuddered, sighed.

Then he was gone.

'You're out of time,' Dawa said. He pointed down the glacier where more of Viking's men had now come into view.

'We need to put at least one big crevasse between us

and them.' Kami observed.

'If you're going to make a break for it, now's the time.' Dawa told us. 'I've got two more clips of ammunition then I'm out. Now go!'

'How will you get away?' I asked.

'This place is a maze,' Dawa said. 'I was always good at hide and seek.'

Crouched down low, we used the cover of a gully to move deeper into the Icefall.

Dawa was returning fire. A scream far back on the glacier told us another of his shots had hit home.

We hit the first of the big crevasses. Our first opportunity to stop Viking in her tracks. There was no time to do a good job of de-rigging the ladder. We simply cut the ropes attaching it to the ice.

Thirty minutes' more climbing. Kami's breathing was laboured. I heard the occasional sob.

I felt tears prick my eyes. I was furious with myself, cursing that I hadn't guessed there would be guards at the top end of the camp.

And Tashi? Had she really escaped with Shreeya? Or had they also been caught by Viking's men?

I heard Kami sob again. The deep shock of Alex's death was only just beginning to hit us both. Bile rose swiftly to my throat and I stopped to retch.

When I looked up, sun had lit up the Icefall. We were surrounded by high séracs, unable to see what was happening behind us.

The ice here was deep blue.

The gunfire had stopped.

Dawa had been awesome. Without him and his courage under fire we never would have made it this far.

'Do you think he escaped?' Kami asked.

I thought of Dawa's confidence, his military skills.

He was a supremely capable person in every way. If anyone could use the terrain down there to dodge Viking, it was him.

'I think so. But what on earth do we do now?' I asked Kami. 'It's only a matter of time before Viking fixes a new ladder.'

He looked at me intently, his dark brown eyes blinking back tears.

'We do the only thing we can,' he said. 'We keep going up.'

CHAPTER 8

Kami and I kept moving into the Icefall. Every time we passed a marker wand we pulled it up and threw it in a crevasse. Anything and everything to keep Viking from following our trail.

We reached the second big ladder crossing. A crevasse that had been christened 'Big Al' by the climbers at Base. I went first, trying not to look down into the depths, the ladder sagging alarmingly with each nervous step.

As soon as Kami had crossed, the two of us started dismantling the ladder. It was more complicated than I had supposed, the ice screws attaching the end of it had been twisted deeply into the body of the glacier and we didn't have the right tool to extract them.

We fumbled at it for a bit with no success.

'We'll just have to cut the ropes again,' Kami suggested. We took our Swiss army knives and started to saw. Not surprisingly, the cords were incredibly tough, and ten minutes of hard work was needed to sever them.

As we worked, we heard voices in the lower part of the Icefall …

'I think they're looking for Dawa,' Kami said.

I prayed silently that they wouldn't find him.

The ladder broke free. We hurriedly pulled it over, stashing it on a flat section of ice and securing it so that it wouldn't get blown away if a storm ran through the Icefall.

Kami stared at the yawning mouth of the crevasse.

'She can't cross that,' he said.

The gaping ice crack was now a second serious barrier to Viking and her men.

At that moment, far below us, we could see the terrorists halted at the first crevasse. Even at this distance, the tall figure of their leader was easily visible.

She screamed something unintelligible in our direction, the shrill sound echoing around the ice towers.

Viking and her men huddled together for some moments, obviously working out their next move.

'You don't think they'll try to find another route?' Kami asked.

'They're not climbers,' I reminded him.

Kami and I kept going; dismantling two further crevasse crossings as we went. One of them was a four-ladder extravaganza across a truly huge split.

The Icefall was a punishing climb, filled with near-vertical steps, false summits and an ever-more complicated and nerve-wracking array of ladder crossings and cliffs.

We started to talk about finding food and shelter at Camp 1. It was a good way of distracting ourselves.

The scale of the place was impressive. And terrifying. We were far from properly equipped, slithering on the ice without any crampon spikes to keep us stable.

What was worse was that in the days since the terror attack had begun there had been no maintenance on the route. The 'Icefall doctors' – the Sherpa team that had the job of fixing the trail – had all rushed down the valley. In the meantime, the crevasses had widened by almost half a metre with the movement of the Khumbu Glacier, in some places stretching the fixed ropes to breaking point, the ladders resting just by the tips of the side rails.

Like me, Kami was suffering emotionally, tears running freely down his cheeks almost every time I looked at him.

The loss of his mentor had knocked him for six. Alex had been like a father to him for the last two years.

'I don't remember Camp 1 being so far,' he said.

I couldn't comment. It was my first time climbing through the Icefall.

But it did seem like a monumental effort, not least because the higher we got, the bigger the crevasses became. Just before reaching the calmer environment of the Western Cwm – the vast valley that guards Everest's southern approach – these deadly voids reach a veritable crescendo of chaos, splitting the surface of the glacier into a bewildering confusion of dramatic drops and life-threatening towers. The route through this maze seemed to have been planned by a suicidal lunatic, passing beneath overhanging cliffs of ice that I knew could collapse at any second.

Suddenly, Kami slipped. He shot down a steep slope and crashed, hard, into some ice blocks at the bottom.

'You OK?' I called.

He nodded but his face was screwed up in pain.

I grabbed one of the fixed ropes and made my way down to him, helping him to rise awkwardly to his feet.

I could see his legs shaking and his breathing was coming very hard.

'My back … ' he muttered.

We resumed the climb but I could see something had changed. Up until the fall, Kami had been impressively strong, his rehabilitated body coping with pretty much everything.

Now he looked fragile, lacking balance. Every step seemed hesitant, but, even though I asked him, he would not admit he was in pain.

Finally we reached flatter ground, and saw a clutch of tents in the distance.

'Camp 1!' Kami gasped.

The tents were spread over a surprisingly large area of the Western Cwm. They were in three main clusters, each group positioned in the hope of minimising avalanche risk from the slopes above.

We unzipped a few and found they were loaded with equipment, provisions and cooking gas. The Sherpa teams had already done a lot of supply carries to this point.

We chose a tent to use as a base, then rested for a while outside it, getting our breath back, our minds catching up with the monumental events of the past twenty-four hours.

Kami brought out the shrine bell, turning it in his hands. I guessed he was thinking about Shreeya.

'Do you think the girls got away?' he said.

'They have to have done,' I replied. 'Or it's all been for nothing.'

We just sat there on the ice, lost in our own thoughts for a while, our bodies recovering after the intense activity of the climb.

'I've got an idea,' Kami said. 'We might find a radio, get in touch with the girls that way.'

'Genius!' I exclaimed. 'Let's get looking.'

We split up, searching the tents one by one.

It felt wrong to be rummaging through other climbers' belongings but we had no choice.

After an hour of scavenging, Kami and I met back at the base tent. Our raid had the required result: we had four radios, each loaded with fully charged batteries.

We found some flat ice to sit on and examined the transmitters. They were simple devices, one grade up from a walkie-talkie.

I snapped a switch and selected the first frequency.

'This is Camp 1 on Mount Everest,' I said. 'Camp 1 on Everest seeking urgent assistance.'

No reply.

'This is Camp 1 on Mount Everest,' I repeated. 'Camp 1 on Everest seeking urgent assistance.'

Nothing.

No matter what frequency we tried the result was the same. Static. With not the slightest hint of a human voice on the other end.

The two of us tried for almost an hour. Finally Kami turned away from his handset. His eyes were hollow.

'You know what, don't you?' Kami said. 'We're being stupid.'

'What do you mean?'

'We were right that there'd be plenty of radios up here,' Kami continued. 'But they're not powerful enough to speak to Kathmandu.'

'Why not?'

'They're just for the mountain. Talking from one camp to another. They're probably not even strong enough to speak to the nearest village.'

I turned the radio over and over in my hands. What Kami was saying made perfect sense. It was infuriating to think that we had the means to transmit, but not far enough to make a difference.

'We could speak to Base Camp,' Kami said bitterly, 'for all the good that would do us.'

I snorted. Viking was the only one with a radio at base.

We kept stubbornly trying on the radios, but no reply came.

A snowstorm came in from the north at 4 p.m. Flakes the size of fingernails began to fall. By five, visibility was down to a few metres and the snow was blowing like the devil.

We retreated to the tent, which was already sagging under the weight of the snow. Good quality sleeping bags were stashed in there, along with a small cooker and plenty of food, all waiting for climbers who would never arrive. Kami zipped up the front and we spent a good half hour sorting out our borrowed equipment so that the space worked for us and not against us.

We cooked up some corned beef hash and chucked in a tin of spaghetti. We were both ravenous after the climb and the pan of food was gone in a flash. Two tins of fruit followed, with a couple of sliced-up Mars bars thrown in for good measure.

'Where do you think the girls are now?' Kami asked. 'You think they're warm and cosy in a nice lodge somewhere?'

'We just have to pray,' I replied. 'Pray with all our hearts that they didn't get caught.'

I shivered as the cold began to bite. It was time to curl up in our sleeping bags.

I doubted I would sleep. Every time I closed my eyes I saw Tashi's face. I forced myself to think about practical stuff, focusing on the radio problem.

If we couldn't get a radio message out, we would rot here until the siege was over, or until Viking found a way to get to us.

'How long can we stay here,' I asked, 'before we go crazy or the altitude gets us?'

'Ten days?' Kami suggested. 'Two weeks at a push.'

We both fell silent.

The very idea of being stuck up here for that length of time, haunted by Alex's violent death, thinking of the girls but without any news, was enough to chill my heart.

'Other options?' I muttered.

'A helicopter would be nice,' Kami laughed sadly.

I nodded, but we both knew the truth; a helicopter pilot would be risking Viking's bullets by flying near Base Camp.

I went out to collect some more ice for melting. We brewed up a litre of tea.

'Alex saved us today,' Kami said as we sipped the warm fluid. 'We never would have made it without him.'

Kami brought out the shrine bell once more, holding it tight to his chest.

'I still believe in the power of the bell,' he said. 'A bad thing has happened but good things can still come.'

He said a Hindu prayer for Alex.

Exhausted by the emotional twists and turns of the day,

we lay down to rest. As we tried to sleep, the radio began to crackle with a new voice, a man, speaking urgently in a foreign language.

'Who's that?' Kami said groggily. 'It sounds like Russian.'

I tried to connect with the mystery broadcaster, but there was no response.

Everything went silent and both of us slipped quickly into sleep.

Nightmares came fast that night. Alex's death ran through my dreams, over and over.

Breakfast was miserable. Lumpy porridge and frozen muesli bars.

We weren't chatting much and we had headaches from the altitude. I guess we were both wishing we had woken to find the whole thing had just been a bad dream.

After we had eaten, Kami came up with an idea.

'How about we climb around the top of the Icefall so we have a line of sight to the lodges at Gorak Shep?' he suggested. 'Then we can try the radio again.'

I nodded. The small settlement was the closest human habitation to Base Camp and the location the girls would have headed for if they had escaped.

We couldn't assume that anyone was still there, of course, they might have evacuated along with everyone else once Viking and her team of thugs had attacked Base Camp. But surely there might be a caretaker or two? Someone had to be looking after the lodges.

We threaded our harnesses on and roped up together. The ground was heavily crevassed and there were no fixed lines heading in the direction we wanted to go.

It was virgin terrain and doubly dangerous as a result. Snow bridges had collected over the top of even the biggest crevasses, unstable platforms that could collapse without warning.

'Keep the rope tight,' Kami warned. We took turns to lead, probing the surface with a ski pole to try and check what was beneath our feet.

Finally we found ourselves on a natural pathway between two absolutely monster crevasses. On either side of us the ice fell away into inky blue-black voids.

'These are the biggest slots I've ever seen,' I told Kami. They had to be 100 metres deep.

An hour of careful traversing took us round the shoulder of Nuptse, far enough that the vantage point changed and the whole of the Khumbu Glacier was stretched out in all its glory.

The many hundreds of tents at Base Camp were also visible, looking deceptively calm and peaceful.

We looked for signs of Viking and her team but the tiny figures moving around were too far away to identify.

I unpacked the radio from my small rucksack and switched it on.

From this vantage point we had an uninterrupted line of vision down to Gorak Shep some twelve miles away. The collection of lodges was just visible to the naked eye, dark dots against the snow. If there was any chance of making contact with the outside world, this was it.

'This is Camp 1 on Everest calling Gorak Shep. Camp 1 on Everest, do you read me?'

We stared at the handset, willing it to crackle into life.

Kami took over. He persisted for twenty minutes with no result, then gave up. Sitting side by side, we shared a couple of chocolate bars.

'I see smoke,' Kami said. He stood uncertainly, shielding his eyes with a hand.

'What?'

'I see smoke at Gorak Shep,' he repeated.

Away in the distance, I saw it too: black fumes were rising from the small hamlet.

'Maybe Viking's men have burned the lodges,' he muttered.

It seemed horribly plausible, I thought. If any military intended to try and wipe out the terror group, Gorak Shep would be the logical place to base an attempt; its destruction meant rescue was unlikely.

My chest went tight. 'She's thought of everything,' I said.

The retreat back to Camp 1 took place in silence. We had been quietly confident our new idea would work but it had utterly failed.

We were out of contact with the world. Locked in a trap of our own making.

As we approached Camp 1, an avalanche peeled off the slope above. The mass of powdered ice raced down the cliff in seconds, billowing out into a substantial cloud. Our tent was blown about a bit but not buried like some of the others.

I rubbed at the icy grit in my eyes, coughing hard.

It was a reminder of the risks. A reminder of the reality of Everest. The clock was ticking and we had to find a way out.

We spent the afternoon in a kind of stupor. The sky was cloudless, allowing the sun to beat down mercilessly on the tent. The Western Cwm is a natural heat trap when no wind is blowing, high-altitude rays radiating off the valley bottom and side walls.

We lit the cooker to boil up some water. It would create

more heat but we had no choice. As we waited, we heard the faint hiss of the radio.

'Base Camp calling Camp 1,' came the call. A woman's voice. 'Base Camp calling Camp 1.'

My guts twisted.

'Viking,' Kami said.

I turned up the volume. Her voice came loud and clear.

'I know you're there,' she said. 'I've heard your radio chat.'

Kami and I exchanged a glance. We had wondered if our calls might be intercepted. She continued to repeat the message.

Then Kami had a thought.

'We might discover something about the girls,' he said.

The temptation to try and get some news about Tashi and Shreeya was too much. Kami picked up the radio.

'This is Camp 1,' he said. 'What do you want?'

'Information. Anatoly Kuzkin and his daughter are up there, yes?'

Kami looked at me in surprise.

'You're wrong,' Kami told her. 'We haven't seen them.'

'We intercepted a radio message last night,' Viking said. 'Anatoly trying to get in touch with his military backup.'

Kami's eyes widened.

'The Russian voice,' he whispered to me. 'Just before

we went to sleep.'

'Tell Anatoly to come down and give himself up,' Viking said. 'And the rest of you with him. None of you can last much longer at that altitude so why not put yourselves out of your misery?'

'Thanks for your offer,' Kami replied calmly. 'But getting shot by a terrorist isn't on my bucket list.'

There was a long pause at the Base Camp end. It seemed likely that Viking was discussing this response with her men. Then the radio hissed into life again.

'So be it,' Viking said. 'We're coming up.'

The line went dead.

I muttered a curse beneath my breath.

Kami slumped back on to his sleeping bag.

'That's the last thing we need,' he said. 'Her and her thugs rebuilding the ladders across the crevasses.'

'We'll have to keep watch from now on,' I agreed.

'Do you really think that was Kuzkin on the radio last night?'

'I don't know.'

I went out of the tent and looked around the camp. There were no signs of life and we had not noticed any footsteps other than our own.

There were plenty of tents we hadn't looked in but

187

to search every one of them was too time consuming to contemplate.

The afternoon wore on. Depression overtook us, corrosive and unsettling. The thought that Viking and her team were setting out to rebuild the route through the Icefall was seriously troubling. I kept wondering how long it would take them.

Could we hide somehow? Could we climb higher to Camp 2? How could we defend ourselves?

The dome of our little tent became a small incubator, a dome-shaped Dacron oven; the two of us baking inside like a couple of Christmas turkeys.

'Open up the back,' Kami gasped. We unzipped the ventilation flaps at the rear of the tent, hoping to create some sort of through-draught.

Not much changed. It was still sweltering, without the smallest wind to cut us a break. We stripped off to T-shirts and shorts and lay on top of the sleeping bags.

'You know, Alex had a premonition he would die if he ever went back to Everest,' Kami said.

'Really?'

'Yes. When we were in the USA for my treatment he started having terrible dreams. Nightmares in which he was buried in an avalanche. Nightmares where he was lost in a storm, stumbling blindly through a white-out. He described it to me in graphic detail. It really messed him up.'

'He wasn't kidding when he said that Everest was his nemesis.'

'He never would have guessed it would be a bullet that … ' Kami couldn't finish the sentence.

'No.'

We were quiet for a while.

Later I told Kami all about Tashi's family and their misfortunes in Tibet at the hands of the Chinese. He asked a hundred questions about the Everest climb Tashi and I had done the previous year to rescue her younger brother.

'That boy Kharma has courage,' Kami smiled. 'I hope I'll meet him one day.'

At 5 p.m. the moment we had been waiting for arrived: the sun dipped behind the ridge. The temperature inside the tent fell by twenty degrees in as many minutes, the chilled air a total delight after the punishing sun.

The cooler temperatures seemed to wake up my mind.

I turned the radio over and over in my hand, wondering if there was any way we could boost the signal.

The stubby antenna got my attention. Suddenly I had a brainwave.

'How about we try and increase the size of the antenna?' I said.

Kami raised himself up, his eyes suddenly aflame.

'Great idea!' he said, nodding. 'But how?'

'Strip copper cable out of the other radios. Try and find some head torches to plunder.'

We took one of the useless radios and prised the casing open. We were soon disappointed. A quick inspection of the interior revealed hardly any copper cable. The workings were printed circuit boards.

'It's hopeless,' Kami sighed. 'Nice idea but it's not going to work.'

The second night at Camp 1 passed without any meaningful sleep, wraithlike bursts of wind ripping down the valley and slapping the wall of the tent as the fabric flexed and crackled.

The longing for peaceful rest became almost too powerful to bear.

'Demons are rising tonight,' Kami said.

He clutched the shrine bell close all through that blustery night, but – like me – totalled just a couple of hours of uneasy sleep.

Next morning we were up just after dawn, searching more of the tents for a decent radio. Camp 1 was a vast area and there were dozens we hadn't yet checked.

Just after 9 a.m. I heard Kami giving out a jubilant whoop.

'Look at this!' he exclaimed.

In his hands was exactly what we needed: a powerful radio with serious range.

We packed the radio and its battery in Kami's bag.

'This is going to change everything,' he said. 'We have to try it right now. Let's get back to that same viewpoint.'

We crossed the crevasse and traversed back across the top end of the Icefall, following the route of the previous day.

A couple of ravens fluttered above us, cawing aggressively.

'They've come up for breakfast,' Kami said wryly.

'I'm not on the menu,' I told him. I compacted some snow in my hands and threw it at one of them.

The birds banked away with an indignant squawk.

We reached the vantage point with the big valley view and unloaded the gear. A glow of hope began to burn inside me.

'Let's connect the battery,' Kami said.

We fumbled with the connector for a few moments,

then worked out how it clicked together.

'Try it!' Kami said.

I switched the radio on and started to broadcast.

'This is Camp 1 on Everest. Camp 1 on Everest. Anybody receiving us?'

We listened in, detecting a change straight away. The static was different now, filled with voices, faint enough that they sounded like they were coming from the moon.

It was encouraging.

Then a voice that wasn't the least bit faint. It was coming in loud and clear. I almost dropped the handset.

'Ryan? This is Tashi and Shreeya. Do you hear me? Ryan, come in!'

'It's the girls!' Kami yelled. We embraced with the joy of the moment. I pressed the button.

'Tashi! It's me! Are you both safe?'

A squeal of delight came from the other end.

'We made it out. We're down in the valley, safe and sound!'

Kami and I beamed at each other. It was the news we had been longing for.

'How about you?' Tashi's voice trembled. 'We heard a lot of shooting after the explosion. Is everyone OK?'

The air seemed to chill. I paused, searching for words

that would not come. Kami reached out and gently took the handset.

'Alex was killed,' he told Tashi. 'Shot. There was nothing we could do to save him.'

'Oh no!'

The line went quiet for a while, then I asked:

'Have you seen Dawa? He saved our lives back there.'

'Yes. He got here yesterday, dehydrated and exhausted but alive.'

'How about Zhanna?'

'A mystery. She hasn't been seen.'

I passed the handset to Kami and he spoke with Shreeya for a while. The conversation was in Nepali but I could sense the tenderness in his words.

When he finished, I got back on the line with Tashi.

'What are you going to do now?'

'We're going down to Kathmandu,' she replied. 'Spread the news about Viking and what she's doing. The more information gets out, the better the chance of international action.'

There was a long pause.

'She can't get to you, can she?'

Kami and I shared a look.

'Hopefully not,' I replied.

I didn't have the heart to tell the girls that Viking was on the way up.

'OK,' Tashi said. 'Do you think we'll be able to talk again tomorrow?'

'Sure,' I told her. 'Let's try at 7 p.m. Yes?'

The signal was cut. We stood in silence, savouring the words we had shared with the girls.

'The gods have cared for them,' Kami said.

'They're out of Viking's clutches,' I said. 'That's all that counts right now.'

We packed the radio away and trekked back to Camp 1 where we began to search the tents for more cooking gas and food.

The final tent we wanted to check was the furthest from our own, a yellow North Face dome, positioned underneath a rock wall about fifty metres away. It was set back from the main group. There were no fixed ropes in this part of the camp so we probed the ground ahead of us, searching for crevasses or other hazards.

We arrived at the tent and I unzipped the front flap. Poking my head in, I got the shock of my life.

Two people were in there.

And the sharp end of an ice axe was pointed right at my face.

Zhanna reached out to pull the ice axe back.

'Put the axe down, Papa,' Zhanna said. 'I know him. It's the English boy, Ryan.'

CHAPTER 9

Kami and I jammed into that little tent to fill the Russians in on all that had happened. Zhanna smiled broadly as she made us tea. Her father looked haggard, his eyes rimmed with red, a far cry from the suave businessman I had seen pictured in the gossip pages.

'How come you're here?' Kami asked.

'I flew in by helicopter with a bodyguard,' Anatoly said. 'We touched down about three miles from Base Camp and trekked in from there. Zhanna's beacon guided us.'

Kami and I exchanged a look. That explained the mysterious helicopter noise we had heard two nights earlier.

'Best moment of my life,' Zhanna said. 'Hearing Papa's voice whispering to me in that tent.'

She put her arms around her father and gave him a hug. It seemed the two of them had put their differences aside.

'Our plan was to take Zhanna out in the helicopter,' Anatoly explained. 'But an explosion lit up the area we were in and we had to double back.'

'That was us!' Kami said. 'We set the tent on fire as a diversion.'

'The terrorists were swarming everywhere. We had one option,' Anatoly said. 'Heading into the Icefall was our only chance.'

'Where's the bodyguard?' I asked.

'He was fatally wounded. We had no choice but to leave him,' Anatoly said. 'Zhanna and I had to keep going – we could see head torches following.'

Kami and I filled the two Russians in on our story. Zhanna's face crumpled when she heard that Alex had been killed.

'That's two deaths down to Viking,' Anatoly said grimly. He didn't expand on the comment but I saw the fixed expression on his face and, in that moment, recognised another side to his character.

Anatoly Kuzkin was not a man to forgive.

We ate together, jammed into that small tent. The food was basic but filling: pre-packed foil sachets of sausage and beans that we boiled up.

It felt good to be with Zhanna and her father. Four people felt an awful lot safer than two, even if one of us was only twelve.

'How much do you know about this woman – Viking?' Anatoly asked.

'We know she hates you,' Kami replied.

'That's an understatement,' Anatoly spat. 'Her organisation has hounded me for years.'

'She's evil,' Zhanna said.

'She's a thorn in my side,' Anatoly continued. 'She's twice attacked my businesses, once in Uzbekistan, once in Siberia. And now this!'

'She made a big announcement about your Indian Ocean mining operation,' I said. 'Is it true that it might have diverted the monsoon?'

'I don't know,' Anatoly replied. He looked away, clearly uncomfortable with the question.

'She's accusing your company of putting the lives of millions of people at risk,' Kami told him. 'She's broadcasting that to the world. Why don't you make a statement to deny it?'

Anatoly went quiet. Zhanna studied her nails. I sensed he was unsure.

'I am a businessman,' Anatoly said. 'I pay my taxes. I employ tens of thousands of people all over the world. If my operations are legal and above board why should I have to justify them to anyone?'

'So her information is wrong?' Kami asked.

'The methane thing could be partly correct,' Anatoly said grudgingly.

Kami seemed about to say something, but he bit his tongue and kept silent. Zhanna went red in the face but also said nothing.

'Global warming is happening everywhere anyway,' Anatoly continued. 'So it's hard to believe that my business is making such a terrible impact.'

The conversation died away. The theme had soured the mood. It was obvious that Anatoly was in a state of denial.

But it was also obvious that Viking's tactics were evil and vicious.

'Maybe you *should* change things, Papa?' Zhanna suddenly said. 'Perhaps the mining really is damaging the world? Maybe you can invest in something better for the environment?

'Of course,' Anatoly replied without conviction. 'I will think about it.'

We ate some dessert. Two tins of apricots and some

almonds that we had found in a tent earlier in the day.

Zhanna wrapped her sleeping bag around her, shivering with the cold.

Finally the conversation turned to our situation.

'OK, so we need to make a plan,' I said, sounding a lot more confident than I felt. 'We can't just wait here like sitting ducks.'

Anatoly scooped the remainder of his food into his mouth. 'How long will it take Viking to fix the crevasses?' he asked.

Kami thought for a few moments. 'It takes about three days to rig the ladders. At least, that's what it takes the Sherpa teams.'

'They probably won't be so fast,' I said. 'So maybe, say … four days.'

'Can your radio contact Kathmandu?' Anatoly asked.

Kami frowned. 'I guess so,' he said. 'We have a good place for a signal at the edge of the Icefall.'

'I will call a helicopter in to rescue us all,' Anatoly said. 'Let's go out at first light and make the call.'

Kami smiled. 'Those are the best words I've heard in a long time,' he said.

'With a bit of luck we'll be out of here by midday tomorrow,' Anatoly said.

I gripped his arm.

'Thank you,' I said, my voice croaky with emotion.

Zhanna embraced her father.

I felt myself suddenly exhausted. It was like a plug had been pulled. The grief and shock about Alex and the nervous energy we had expended over the last few days had left me shattered.

Kami and I decided it was time to get back to our tent.

'Things are looking hopeful for us now,' Kami said as we trekked back across the ice. 'Anatoly will be as good as his word.'

A sudden gust of wind blew across the camp. The tents rattled with the impact.

I still had a pang of doubt. Would the helicopter companies really want to risk their aircraft at this altitude? Especially while the siege was ongoing?

Wind was one thing. Bullets were quite another.

We crashed out as darkness fell.

The next morning we walked to the top of the Icefall. Kami was limping a bit after his accident but he still got there first.

I heard him groan.

'Come and take a look,' he said.

Part way down the Icefall, a group of men were working on one of the crevasses, fixing ladders across the gaps. *Much* higher than we had imagined. I muttered a curse.

'They must have found a stash of ladders at Base Camp,' Kami said. 'It looks like they've been at it all night. They've only got three big crevasses to go.'

My stomach churned. The men were more than halfway up. Five out of the eight crevasses we had stripped were now bridged again.

Viking was keeping her promise. And now the chase was on.

'We've been too complacent,' I said. 'They'll be here in hours at this rate.'

'We should have checked,' Kami said bitterly. 'We could have seen their head torches if we had come out to look in the night.'

As we stood there, a big bank of misty cloud rolled across our position.

How soon would they get to us? I wondered. *Would they keep working non-stop? Even if we hurried up to Camp 2 further up the valley, would we wake up tomorrow to the sound of gunfire?*

The cloud thickened. Soon Viking and her team were

lost to view.

'No helicopter this morning,' Kami said bleakly. 'The visibility is too low.'

'Then we've only got one move we can make,' I muttered.

We hurried back to the tents where a groggy Zhanna and Anatoly were just waking up.

'Get your rucksacks ready,' Kami told them urgently. 'Viking is on her way up and we're leaving for Camp 2 right now.'

'C ... C ... Camp 2?' Anatoly stammered. 'How close are they?'

'Close enough that we have no choice,' I told him.

'What about the heli ... ?' Zhanna's voice faltered as she saw the cloud.

'No one's going to be flying today,' Kami said.

We headed back to our tent and kitted up. Kami asked me to lace up his boots; his back was too sore to do it himself.

When I was ready, I hurried back to the Russians. Anatoly was deathly pale.

'My head,' he complained. 'It's been aching the whole night.'

We brewed them a quick cup of tea and left Camp 1.

My mind turned over and over as we began the trek. Kami was increasingly fragile after his slip in the Icefall. Then there was an overwhelming feeling of responsibility for Zhanna and her father.

A twelve-year-old girl. A man who – so far as I knew – had never been on any kind of mountain before. Zhanna was headstrong. Anatoly was showing every sign of being totally out of his depth. Not a good combination if things got heavy up there.

Would the two Russians listen to Kami and me if a difficult decision had to be made?

Everest was waiting for us. Unpredictable, ever dangerous, and we *really* weren't prepared.

Anatoly was slow. Dead slow. Altitude had dulled his whole body and it took him half an hour just to walk out of the Camp 1 zone.

The route began to follow the climbing trail. Pushing slowly but determinedly further up the valley. The day was overcast, the sky glowering with a sinister grey sheen.

My rucksack was shockingly heavy, crushing my shoulders. Kami and I had deliberately taken more to give Zhanna and Anatoly lighter packs. I reckoned mine weighed twenty-five kilos at least.

We were carrying plenty of food and cooking gas, mainly because we had no idea how much would be stashed at Camp 2.

The wind was playing, kicking up small plumes of powdered ice.

I watched Zhanna as she put one foot in front of the other, her shoulders set, her pace strong.

Then I grinned. Maybe I had got it all the wrong way around. It might be us that would be relying on *her*.

A cascade of ice blocks crashed down the slope just a stone's throw in front of us.

'Why are you taking us this way?' Anatoly grumbled. 'We can be killed by an avalanche here.'

'It's the only path,' Kami replied. 'There are too many crevasses on the other side.'

I looked up. The valley sides were loaded with threat. Hanging glaciers the size of shopping malls defied gravity as they clung to sheer slopes above us. Spindrift avalanches were coming down constantly, lightweight snow blown down in vast quantities that could bury us if we strayed too close to the edges of the valley.

From time to time the clatter and rattle of falling boulders echoed across the valley.

There was no opportunity to relax.

We were the first climbers to take the route for many days. The fixed ropes had mostly been buried in deep snow and we had to pull them out and shake them free. We lost plenty of time excavating them from the grip of the snow.

It was hard drill but I was glad to be moving. Every step we took kept us a step ahead of Viking.

I figured that there was a chance she and her team would not be able to follow beyond Camp 1. Altitude sickness could strike them.

If all went well, we could hide in Camp 2 and wait for her to retreat.

'I'm seriously worried about Anatoly,' Kami told me, as we stopped to share a hot chocolate from the flask. 'He's grumpy as an old goat and that's a sign his altitude sickness could be getting worse.'

'I agree,' I replied.

I stared at the route ahead, taking in the impact of the scene, the incredible scale of this, the highest valley in the world. Camp 2 was at the far end of the natural amphitheatre, a collection of about fifty tents, which looked half buried in snow.

It was no place for a human being.

'Looks lethal up there,' I said.

'The shrine bell will guide us,' Kami said. 'It will keep us safe.'

His words were calming and reassuring.

I couldn't resist casting my eyes even higher. Way above the col, we could now see the final ridge of Everest, a knife-edge switchback rising steeply to the heavens. The summit was out of sight, obscured by a swirling mass of cloud.

Zhanna and Anatoly trudged wearily up to our position half an hour later. Anatoly fell to the ground like he'd been hit with an axe.

'Do people really call this a sport?' he gasped.

'Headache,' Zhanna said. We gave them both a paraceta-mol and some fluid.

We ticked off an hour of downtime. Body recovery. It went like a flash as we gradually felt the crystal sharpness of the invading cold, our muscles seizing up with inactivity.

From time to time we glanced nervously back to Camp 1.

Then it was time to go.

'Get up!' Zhanna told her father. When he didn't move she reached out and helped him to his feet.

It took a while for our legs to snap back into the rhythm. Setting off is always a shaky time when body tissue is chilled.

'I feel like I'm switched off,' Anatoly said.

My knees ached like crazy but Kami and I soon pulled ahead.

Kami was pensive.

'We should have brought oxygen cylinders with us on this section,' he said, 'for Anatoly.'

'I couldn't carry any more,' I told him. My rucksack already felt at the top end of what I could bear.

'What if they chase us up higher? It might end up being a big problem,' Kami said. 'Normally we'd have Sherpa high-altitude porters helping to carry the bottles. How are we going to manage when we're up in the zone where we all need the O_2?'

'We'll just have to carry our own bottles,' I said.

Easy words. But at eight kilos for each full bottle I guessed the reality could be devastating.

'Every gram counts up there,' Kami said, doubtfully. 'And if you look at Anatoly now ... '

He left the statement hanging.

The Russian was a good 500 metres behind us already, taking just three faltering steps with each burst of activity before slumping over his ice axe and resting for long minutes.

Zhanna waited by his side. Ever patient.

We started the traverse, crossing the entire glacier to

the northern flank, following the red marker wands that poked out of the drifted snow here and there.

Finally, ahead of us was Camp 2.

Camp 2 was another ghost camp devoid of climbers. Like Camp 1, it was placed strategically, on the downhill side of ridges and humps that might divert the power of an avalanche from the slopes above.

'There have been a lot fewer load carries to this one,' Kami observed. 'We might struggle to find food.'

We waited in the wind shadow of a solitary boulder as Zhanna and her father caught up.

Most of the domes had been buried. We found a couple of avalanche shovels and began to dig two tents clear.

'It's lonely being up here like this,' Kami said. 'Camps are normally full of life. There should be voices, laughter.'

Kami was right. The camp had a melancholy air of abandonment. It was hard not to feel depressed as we gradually dug out our frozen homes.

Zhanna, typically, just kept scraping off the snow without complaint. The harder the work was, the more she seemed to relish it.

An hour of shovelling freed up the two tents. My chest

and shoulder muscles were aching like crazy. We had run out of fluid hours before, so we were all seriously dehydrated. We gathered ice for melting and sat there with our tongues stuck to the roofs of our mouths.

While we waited for the stove to melt the ice, I went out to check the view down the valley. I could see people moving at Camp 1. Viking had made it, but we were still one climbing day ahead.

The crucial question was: *could she go higher?*

If she pursued us further we would have no choice but to move up to Camp 3.

Zhanna had been on a food raid around the camp, burrowing into buried tents like a little mole, scoring a hotchpotch of packet noodles, corned beef and potato powder.

'I will cook!' Anatoly announced. I think he felt guilty about holding us up earlier and it was a sign that he was feeling a bit stronger.

After we had eaten, there was the nervous wait for 7 p.m., our agreed radio rendezvous with Tashi. We walked up to some higher ground near the camp to try and get a signal, but all we heard was static.

Try as we might, we couldn't get through.

We trudged back to the tent and I couldn't help feeling blue. 'I wish we could have spoken to the girls,' I told Kami.

'Don't feel too sad,' he said. He brought the shrine bell out of his rucksack and turned it fondly in his hands. 'Positive thought is important. One year ago I was lying on my back. Paralysed. But I never had negative thoughts. Now I am back on Everest and expecting a baby with Shreeya.'

'You always put others first,' I told him. 'Never felt sorry for yourself even when things must have seemed helpless.'

'I still worry about Shreeya. I wonder if she and the baby are OK. I just have to pray everything will be fine.'

I thought about the girls, heading down into the mayhem of Kathmandu. They would be there in a few days. Would the riots be over by then?

They were both tough; I had seen that for myself. And they had lots of friends they could call on in the city.

Nevertheless, I was besieged by dark thoughts that night. They seemed to come as part of the package when strong winds hit the mountain.

Would Kami have the strength to go higher? How far could he push his newly restored body? What about Zhanna and her father?

If any of them hit the wall there would be no chance of rescue.

And what about me? I still felt the occasional twinge in my arm from the climbing accident. I wondered if it would let me down if we had to go higher. Hauling on the fixed ropes would require all my strength.

Halfway through the night I went out to check that Viking and her team weren't on their way up. There was just enough moonlight to see down the valley.

No movement. The climb through the Icefall must have exhausted them.

I fell asleep to the repetitive crackling noise of the tent fabric as it was pummelled by fierce winds.

By dawn we were awake, rubbing our fingers and toes over the heat of the gas fire to get some circulation going.

We met outside the tents, my head aching from the thin air. The wind was from the north. It already felt like it was going to be an extremely cold day.

The good news was that Anatoly and Zhanna had both slept well. They looked more alert than the previous day; a sign that they were acclimatising.

Then I felt Kami grip my arm. He pointed down the valley.

Back at Camp 1 there was movement amongst the tents. Then, four climbers walked out.

'They're coming,' Kami said.

'Damn that woman!' Anatoly exclaimed.

I looked at Kami. We both knew there was no choice now.

This was a poker game and Viking was calling our bluff. They were armed. We didn't have a single weapon.

We had to continue up. Camp 3 was our next refuge.

'No time to lose,' Kami told the Russians.

Anatoly looked up the Lhotse Face, his jaw clenching as he saw how far it was to the next camp.

'Seriously?' he murmured. 'I'm not sure I … '

Zhanna put her hand on his shoulder.

'We can do it,' she said. 'The only alternative is giving ourselves up.'

Anatoly nodded, but his eyes were glazed.

I switched on the radio while we waited for Anatoly to get ready. It was a terrible line but I managed to get Tashi for a few seconds, long enough to tell her that Viking and her men were still on our trail.

'I will look into other options,' she promised. 'You might be able to go over the col and escape on the other side.'

The connection died. Thirty minutes later, we left the relative safety of the camp.

Tashi's words chased around my head.

Escape on the other side of the mountain.

It was an intriguing idea.

CHAPTER 10

Camp 2 quickly became a distant memory. We were trekking up to the vast wall at the end of the valley. The closer we got, the more I became awed by its scale and gradient. It didn't just look punishing. It looked a total epic.

Deep inside a voice was starting to question: *Can you hack it? Even the flat terrain here is exhausting. The air is so thin and it's getting thinner. Better if you admit defeat now.*

Self-doubt. Self-perpetuating. Feeding on its own weakness.

'Everest is a mind game,' Kami said, as we rested at the bottom of the face. 'And the worst thing you can do is look up.'

Zhanna and Anatoly trekked to our position. Anatoly

had put on too many layers that morning and was now complaining about being too hot. He stripped off his outer wind suit and stuffed it in his pack. Zhanna sipped at her water bottle, preferring to stand rather than slump on the ice as the three of us had done.

'Mountain beaten you already?' she asked.

I had to grin. Her sparky attitude showed no signs of relenting even as our situation worsened.

'Don't be arrogant,' Kami told her. 'The gods will teach you a lesson if you get too cocky.'

Zhanna tossed her head. 'We'll see.'

We began the climb up the Lhotse Face, legs and arms protesting as we hit the steeper terrain. Our pace crashed to a crawl, each kick of the crampons gaining us just a few centimetres of height.

We hit the fixed ropes. Kami taught Zhanna and Anatoly how to do the changeover from one rope to the next. They were fast learners and I was pleased to see Zhanna clipping her karabiner around the line with great care. The slightest slip would be fatal up here.

'This reminds me of the climb to the North Col on the Tibetan side,' I told Kami.

'I hated this slope the first time I did it,' he replied. 'And I don't feel any different now.'

Step. Breathe.

Wonder where the strength will come from for the next step.

Step. Breathe. Repeat.

Demons inhabit these steep slopes. Maximum doubts come at a time of maximum pain. The mind and body seem to become divorced as the brutal climb goes on. The body has questions for the mind and they seem entirely reasonable.

Why are you doing this to me?

When is this going to end?

Of course the mind cannot reply. Often it has doubts of its own and the question of when it will all end is an impossible one to answer beyond the obvious:

The harder you work, the quicker this pain will stop.

To which the body replies:

That's what you've been telling me all day!

It's a very strange game.

Gradually, Kami began to fall behind. I waited from time to time for him to catch up, very much aware that his newly restored body was now being put to the ultimate test.

'I had forgotten the true size of this mountain,' he gasped.

'Me too,' I replied. My Everest climb with Tashi seemed like a lifetime ago.

Zhanna and Anatoly were even further back. It was

obvious the young Russian girl had to slow her pace to match her father's. From time to time we heard the silvery clear tone of her voice, urging him on.

My mind wandered. I thought of Tashi and Shreeya, hoping that they would both be OK down in Kathmandu amidst the riots and chaos.

At midday we found a flattish scrap of rocky ground. It wasn't much bigger than a ping-pong table but it was enough for a break. We stopped to refuel, get some calories inside us. Barely a word passed between the four of us as we munched on muesli bars and dried dates.

Anatoly took just a tiny bite. He had no appetite at all. Always a brooding presence, his brow was furrowed as he stared out across the vastness of the valley.

He had a small electronic altimeter in his gloved hand. He turned it over and over, like it was a talisman, a lucky charm.

I would have liked to know what was churning around in his head. But he wasn't the kind of guy for idle chit-chat. And we were pretty well brain-dead from the grind of the climb.

Viking and three men were still coming up the valley.

They maintained a steady pace but it was obvious they were suffering just as we were. They stopped frequently, lying prone on the ice to rest, four little dark dots lost in the immensity of the valley.

Viking was in the front position. Faster than the rest.

'She doesn't stop,' Zhanna said. 'She's like a machine.'

A beeping noise announced a radio call coming in. My heart raced as I heard Tashi on the line:

'I might have an escape option for you,' she said, urgently. 'I got on the internet and did some research on the expeditions on the other side this year. Our friends the Canadians are there again, Ryan. You remember the leader, Christophe?'

'Sure. A really nice guy.'

My mind raced. Tashi had opened up an interesting possibility. It made perfect sense to evacuate from the other side of the mountain if we had a friendly team waiting to help us.

'I contacted him,' Tashi said. 'He's agreed to help if you decide to do it. He's fixing ropes to the summit for his own team anyway and they could leave them in place for you. When you get down to the valley floor they could meet you and help you dodge the checkpoints to get back to Kathmandu.'

'It's an amazing idea,' I said. 'But you're forgetting something; we'd have to go via the summit!'

'If Viking keeps following, it's your only real option,' Tashi insisted. 'Otherwise you're trapped.'

The radio link suddenly faded, then went dead.

It started to snow. Gentle, wispy flakes brushed against the hood of my wind suit.

'There's work to be done,' Kami said.

Everest decided to set us an extra test that day. The angle of the slope grew more acute as we continued up the Lhotse Face. Frequent slides of spindrift swept down and coated us.

I was thinking constantly about Tashi's escape plan, my mind churning over her words.

Kami and I also talked the strategy through.

'I don't think Anatoly can make it much higher,' Kami said. 'Certainly not to the summit.'

A boulder thudded down the face only metres in front of us. To my oxygen-starved brain it looked like a meteorite crashing to earth.

'I see Camp 3!' Kami said.

I rubbed a frozen smear of ice from my goggles and stared up the slope.

'Still quite far,' I said glumly. The tents seemed miles away.

'Two more hours and we'll be there,' Kami promised.

We scraped out a platform to rest on. I found myself drifting off into a glorious power nap, my head snapping forward with a start as Kami nudged me awake.

I could have slept all day and night right there.

It wasn't two hours to the next camp in the end. It was closer to four. Anatoly was managing no more than five steps between every long rest by the time he hit the last climb to the camp.

'We are only as strong as the weakest link,' Kami said.

'Same goes for Viking,' I replied.

Viking's little four-man convoy had been whittled away by the rigours of the day. One of her team had turned back halfway along the valley.

I watched as Anatoly puked up on the ice. Even Zhanna's constant encouragement couldn't cheer him up.

Camp 3 was in a bad state. Left without maintenance, the tents had not fared well. Many had been hit by wind, yanking out the ice pegs that anchored them, and a few were totally flattened, the fabric flapping sadly, rips opening up.

There were only two tents that could be made habitable.

Kami and I unpacked our belongings, happy to see there were a few spare oxygen cylinders stacked at the back of the tent.

We jammed into the Russian tent at supper time, sharing the oxygen canisters and cooking up a saucepan of tuna and tomato pasta.

'I've got an idea,' Anatoly said. 'How about we destroy everything here when we leave – all the tents, throw the cooking stuff down the slope? That will stop Viking.'

'It won't stop her,' Kami said, 'it will kill her.'

Anatoly shrugged. 'So be it,' he said.

Zhanna's eyes narrowed. Then she looked away.

'We might need those things ourselves if we have to come back down this way,' I pointed out.

We didn't have the energy to debate it further. Kami and I left for our own tent.

We slept with the oxygen masks on that night. At more than 7,000 metres up, we were too high to be breathing unaided. The hiss of gas was reassuring and the extra trickle of oxygen kept us warm, even if the masks were uncomfortable where they pressed against the face.

Calls of nature were distracting or even dangerous. We had no pee bottles so a trip out on to the ice was necessary. The temptation to risk it without crampons was overwhelming.

I thought about Anatoly's idea as I wrapped myself up in my sleeping bag. Destroying a safe refuge on Everest went against every shred of mountain sanity. Ethically, it was off the scale of inhuman behaviour. This camp was a haven, a shelter from the storm, a place to escape the elements. What right did we have to wreck it?

Viking and her men would never survive a night in the open.

'A part of me thinks Anatoly is right,' Kami said, 'but doing it would be murder. Terrible karma.'

'They'd die,' I agreed. 'As sure as if we shot them.'

Our conversation petered out as the wind began to rise.

We fell quiet, both thinking our own thoughts as we drank cup after cup of restoring sweet tea.

Later we both slipped into a fitful sleep, tormented by thirst in the early hours as our dehydrated bodies begged for fluid.

At 4.30 a.m. Zhanna unzipped our tent.

'Time to go,' she said. 'I can see head torches leaving Camp 2.'

I poked my head out of the front and saw two pinpricks of light bobbing far below us. Two, not three.

Viking was pushing hard. Thanks to her weapons she still had the strategic advantage. But another of her men had obviously quit.

How much longer could she keep going?

And how long would it be before Anatoly reached his limit?

The morning passed in a haze of hard work. We cut our resting time down to the absolute minimum, just a ten-minute break every two hours.

As we gasped our way up the Lhotse Face, Everest pulled one of her surprising mood changes, blitzing the slope with a powerful and unrelenting sun.

The previous day had felt like the Arctic. Now the vibe was more semi-tropical, our body temperatures gradually rising as the radiation blasted off the snowy slope and straight on to our overdressed bodies.

'My face is frying,' Zhanna complained. We were short of glacier cream, having to ration just one tube between us.

I gave her my blob of UV protection, accepting that my face would be sun blistered by the end of the day.

The intense power of the sun did not relent for a moment. We grabbed a few crackers and a chunk of cheese for lunch, then got going as quickly as we could, desperate to escape the heat. By mid-afternoon, the snow was wet and heavy as liquid cement, slipping down the slope in steeper places in a continuous slow-motion avalanche.

It meant every step was even more of a battle.

'My boots are wet through,' Kami said. 'This stuff is getting everywhere.'

I was suffering the same. The snow up here had the unwelcome knack of working its way into every nook and cranny, penetrating our gaiters and soaking our socks.

My calf and thigh muscles were locking up into cramps whenever I stopped. We had run out of fluid halfway up the ropes. My mouth was seriously dry, an unmistakable sign of dehydration that even my altitude-dulled brain couldn't fail to recognise.

The lining of my throat had taken a pounding from the dry air. A slight sore throat had morphed over the previous couple of days into a painful inflammation that made swallowing a dreaded event.

We had abandoned our two-hour climbing routine. The need for rest was impossible to ignore. Stops now came every ten minutes, the delicious sensation of resting more intensely enjoyable each time. The view was opening up beneath us, with the entire arena of the western valley laid out in spectacular fashion.

Viking was halfway up to Camp 3. Her fellow climber

was weakening; he slipped further behind every time we looked.

'That guy's going to give up,' Kami said with some satisfaction.

'Maybe,' Anatoly said, 'but she won't.'

I had to agree with his assessment. Viking's venom for Anatoly was beyond anything.

Onward. Upward. We hit a series of stony sections. Not quite vertical but steep enough to need some scrambling. The rock was horribly loose, fragmenting and sliding at the slightest touch.

'Don't trust these ropes,' Kami advised.

The steps were fixed with ancient lines of unknown origin. Some of them even looked like hemp, the rope that was used in the 1950s.

Kami and I went up first. Then Zhanna set about the biggest of the steps, attacking it far too fast and looking unstable with every move.

'Take it slow!' I called down. 'I'll give you a hand over the crest.'

She got into a mess. The ropes were conspiring against her, tangling dangerously around her boots.

After ten minutes of slipping and sliding, she reached the top of the step. She gave an exhausted little cry and hugged me.

'That was painful,' she gasped. 'How much further to go?'

She stared towards the col, wiping her goggles to remove a layer of thin ice that had collected.

'Oh. Still some way,' Kami said.

Anatoly was the last to come up. He was gasping heavily by the time he got to us, forcing us to rest for twenty minutes or so until his breathing got back under control.

Reaching the wind-hardened ice below the col was a welcome relief. The pleasure of planting steps on a surface that did not slide perpetually downwards seemed an incredible bonus.

'I remember this place,' Kami said. 'The Geneva Spur. It was a nightmare last time.'

Kami's memory was spot on. It was a nightmare. Complications of the undulating terrain forced us up a rising slope, obliging us to climb higher than the col in order to get to it.

I didn't check my watch but it seemed to take a massive chunk of the day to climb that punishing section alone. Certainly the heat was still extreme and there were no clouds around to tame the searing power of the sun. Every time I bent over my ice axe – wanting to quit, feeling the sweat trickle down the edge of my mask, wanting the pain to stop – Kami was there with a few encouraging words.

'You can keep going, Ryan.'

I could see the glimmer of a smile in his eyes, deep behind the mirrored lens of his goggles. He was a powerhouse. Even though he was still limping from the slip in the Icefall. His strength gave me strength.

The sun sank behind the ridge. A cutting wind began to blow, cold enough to slice through my weather gear and chill me to the bone. I saw that Zhanna was shivering too.

The snow conditions changed with the shift of temperature.

The higher we climbed on the Lhotse Face, the more I became aware of avalanche threat. The snowpack had been swept by a strong wind in the night, creating a crust on top.

'Windslab,' Kami said. 'Very dangerous.'

He pushed the tip of his ice axe into the crust, causing it to break up into angular pieces that skittered down the slope.

'We need to get on to the col as quickly as we can.'

We reached another section of fixed ropes, possibly from the previous season as they were mostly windblown, eroded against the rocks in places to a fuzzy thread, offering extremely dubious protection.

Then we reached the high point. At long last we could look over the col.

I felt an intense desire to shout or scream or mark the moment with something other than this mute sensation of utter exhaustion.

Kami came to my side.

'Plenty of tents,' he said with satisfaction.

We could take our pick of the forty or so that had been erected there.

Naturally we chose the closest tent to our position, tumbling into the cramped, sagging little dome like it was the most luxurious mansion on earth. There were a few personal belongings in there, some spare thermal clothing and a stash of food.

Zhanna and Anatoly chose a similar dome nearby.

The cooker snapped into life with a reassuring rush of combusted gas. We played paper, scissors, stone to decide who would go out to collect the ice for melting down.

I lost. Kami patted my back. Massive willpower was needed to get me back out of that tent on the hunt for clean snow and ice. A piercing wind had started to blow, forcing high-pitched whistling tunes from the larger rocks. The business end of my ice axe chipped away for ages before I had the bag filled.

I shared the ice with our Russian friends. They didn't have the energy to come out of their tent.

Kami and I started the melting process. My thirst demanded results far faster than the cooker could deliver. Kami was the same. Our throats were parched.

Kami shook me awake when the pot was boiling. Still sitting up, I had fallen into a deep sleep.

I threw in a couple of mint teabags as soon as the water was boiled, and the tent filled with the delicious aroma.

My sore throat was still troubling me. At the same time a 'Khumbu cough' had flared up. I was coughing incessantly, a dry hack, which I really could have done without.

We had canned fish and beans in our food supply, but a sachet of mushroom soup was the only thing we felt like eating. That and cheese crackers. Kami took on cooking duties, stirring out the powdery lumps and trying not to fall asleep on the job.

The gas was getting low. It took Kami over an hour to make a single tepid cupful for each of us. I forced the soup down; eyes watering as each mouthful cut a path down my inflamed throat.

Then came sleep, but it didn't last long. I had a heart-ripping nightmare; a body lay buried in the snow. As I stumbled towards it, some gruesome instinct made me brush away the cover of ice.

The face I uncovered was my own, eyes frozen open.

I woke with a cry of terror, which seemed loud enough to set off avalanches all over the Western Cwm.

Kami didn't even stir.

Shocked awake, all hope of sleep was lost. I kept my head torch on for comfort, staring at the ice crystals spreading on the inside of the tent.

Dawn came slowly, a creeping grey-blue light brushing against the exterior wall of the tent. I was fuzzy in the head after a night of no sleep. We forced down a mug of coffee each, the caffeine giving my brain a welcome jolt.

When we emerged we found Zhanna tinkering with her crampons outside her tent. Anatoly was standing some distance away, by the lip of the col, staring down the Lhotse Face.

'Come and look at this,' he called.

We all walked over.

'Viking,' he said. 'Halfway up already.'

'And alone,' Zhanna added.

The four of us stared down at the lonesome figure climbing about 500 metres from our position. What had happened to her last remaining team member?

Then we saw some tiny figures down in the valley,

hurrying at top speed to Camp 1.

'All her men are pulling out,' I observed. 'They've obviously decided to cut their losses.'

'Why doesn't she stop?' Zhanna said. 'Isn't she exhausted as well?'

'In your dreams!' Anatoly replied. 'That woman doesn't know exhaustion. Hatred will keep her moving. And she will be armed to the teeth.'

Kami brought out some biscuits and passed them round. Next time we looked back we saw that Viking was moving even faster, hauling herself up the fixed lines with powerful, rhythmic thrusts of her arms.

It seemed inevitable that she would catch us. And equally inevitable that bloodshed would be the result.

Anatoly's head slumped down. He looked like a beaten man. Then he began to speak.

'There's only one way to handle this,' Anatoly said slowly. 'I'm going back to talk to her.'

I saw the colour drain from Zhanna's face.

'Don't do it,' she said. '*Please*, Papa.'

'I can't go any higher, Zhanna. I have to end this one way or the other. I won't have you put in danger any longer.'

Anatoly and Zhanna embraced.

'But … ' the word caught in Zhanna's throat.

'She will catch us whatever we do,' Anatoly said. 'This is a confrontation that has to happen, so it might as well happen now.'

They held each other tight for long moments.

'I will tell her I will stop the mining,' he added. 'Let us then see what her next move will be.'

He turned to Kami and me.

'Thank you for everything you have done,' he told us.

He embraced us both in turn.

'OK,' he said. 'I'm going.'

CHAPTER 11

Anatoly trekked out along the fixed ropes.

Zhanna stifled a sob. I could see her eyes welling up.

He moved purposefully across the Geneva Spur and began to descend the upper slopes of the Lhotse Face.

Viking had stopped.

'She is waiting,' Kami said. 'She has seen Anatoly coming down.'

As Anatoly continued his descent we saw the weather was changing. Cloud was massing in the cwm, creeping inexorably up the Lhotse Face. After fifteen minutes Viking was swallowed up.

Twenty minutes later we lost visual contact with Anatoly. Zhanna became increasingly anxious, pacing back and forth, wondering if we should follow her father down the ropes.

'This is such a mistake,' Zhanna said, her voice strained with tears. 'He shouldn't have gone.'

Deep within the rising plume of cloud we heard a chilling sound.

A single gunshot.

The world seemed to hold still. It seemed even the rush of wind was put on pause for a few milliseconds. Then a new sound began on high.

The mountain shook. Séracs were collapsing up on the Lhotse Face.

Zhanna screamed, a raw cry of primal fear.

Millions of tons of ice were on the move, accelerating, hurtling down the face in an awesome tsunami of ice. The shockwave of the pistol shot had triggered an avalanche that was heading for Anatoly and Viking.

Our position was out of the strike line, on the edge of the col.

Kami held Zhanna in his arms.

The rising weather system swallowed the avalanche. The billowing leading edge consumed by the cloud. There was no cry from within. No shout. Just the deep roar of the cascading ice, the tremor of the ground beneath our feet.

Gradually the rumble faded. The world was perfectly quiet, perfectly white.

'Papa!' Zhanna gasped. Acting on instinct, she moved towards the lines. Heading down. Towards the scene of the avalanche. Kami grabbed for her shoulder, but she dodged underneath his arm and ran for the first of the fixed ropes.

'Zhanna!' Kami yelled.

She moved incredibly fast, her crampon spikes kicking up tiny spurts of ice with each step. Kami followed at a half run, his breath coming fast.

'Zhanna!' I cried. 'You mustn't go down there, the ropes will be ripped away!'

She ignored my call. I followed them both, watching as she reached the edge of the Geneva Spur, climbed out across the rocky ledges, balancing above crazy drops while striding from one foothold to another.

A few tangles of ropes were still in place up here.

'Clip on!' I screamed.

Zhanna clipped her sling on to the line, but, if anything, it only seemed to encourage her to move faster. Her karabiner was singing as it flew down the rope.

We entered the cloud. Visibility fell to just a few metres.

Zhanna was swallowed up in the white haze. It was unthinkable to let her descend alone. We could only follow.

Down that lethal face. Losing precious height we had gained. Across the rockfall zone next to the spur.

It wasn't hard to spot the area the avalanche had swept.

'The ropes have gone!' Kami yelled. 'You must stop!'

The entire snowpack had been scrubbed off the face. In places we were moving across bare bedrock, our crampon spikes scraping and skittering as steel sparked against stone.

The young Russian did not stop. She was now totally unprotected. One slip could send her cartwheeling down the lethal slopes of the Lhotse Face. Directly beneath our position there were ice cliffs and vertical drops of a hundred metres or more.

'Use your axe!' Kami's voice was hoarse with shouting.

Zhanna ignored him. Her ice axe swung freely in her hand. In that position she would never be able to arrest a fall.

'You're going too low,' I bellowed.

There were no ropes to guide us. And the avalanche had changed the terrain. Zhanna was going on instinct, heading for the last place we had seen her father and Viking.

The avalanche had to have swept them down. I could understand her logic.

But there were crevasses hidden beneath our feet. This crazy descent was taking us into deadly and unpredictable terrain.

Kami stopped, bent double, his body unable to keep up with the pace.

'You think it's possible they can still be alive?' I asked.

'Anything is possible,' he puffed. 'Think about me. I survived the same.'

I continued on Zhanna's trail, pondering on the chances. *Could Anatoly and Viking have survived the avalanche? Surely they would be buried?*

In which case, the clock was ticking.

I caught Zhanna up. I had no spare breath for conversation. We found a couple of tents, ripped up and shredded.

'Must have been the site of Camp 3.' Zhanna's voice was sharp with fear.

Oxygen bottles were strewn about the slope. A sleeping bag was torn up and gutted, the feather down spewing into the blustering wind like a ripped-apart bird.

Zhanna stared down the slope, peering into the seething mass of cloud. Dark shapes were down there but it was impossible to tell what they were.

'Papa!' Zhanna yelled. 'Call if you hear me!'

No reply.

'What can we do?' she asked me. Her voice cracked with emotion. 'Tell me, *please*!'

'There's only one hope,' I told her. 'They could have been

swept into a crevasse just below our position. If they went the whole distance down the slope then there's no chance.'

'I'm going down,' Zhanna said between sobs. 'Let's follow the avalanche track.'

She turned, front-pointing down the icy slope. I was happy to see she used her ice axe this time, thrusting it in deep and securing herself with every step.

'OK, I'm coming with you.' I turned to face the slope.

'There must be clues,' Kami said breathlessly. 'Look for pieces of clothing. Anything.'

About fifty metres beneath the debris we found a flat balcony. It wasn't very wide but it was protected by a slender crevasse, which had been filled almost to the brim by the falling snow and ice.

I wished the cloud would lift so we could see more.

'Let's check it,' I said.

Zhanna jumped into the crevasse. She found a partly buried object right away, pulling it free with a triumphant gasp.

'That's the axe he was using, yes?' Zhanna said.

I examined the manufacturer's logo. She was right.

'Quickly!' Zhanna cried. I joined her as she started to probe the snow.

I was half hoping, half dreading to feel a human form

beneath the ice, the telltale yield of a body.

Nothing. Only rock-hard ice blocks that were now setting like concrete.

Using our axes, we chipped away.

Ten minutes. No result.

The cloud began to clear. I decided to look over the edge of the platform. Another crevasse was hidden below. A crumpled figure lay within it.

'I see him!' I yelled.

Anatoly had been swept further by the sliding debris.

'Papa!' Zhanna cried.

We climbed down fast. Anatoly was ominously still. He was covered in a thin layer of debris but his head was clear of the ice.

We knelt at his side.

'He's breathing!' Zhanna cried.

Kami took a fleece from his rucksack and placed it under the Russian's head.

Anatoly uttered a groggy gasp. Zhanna put her head against his shoulder, her arm cradling him.

'Papa? Where are you hurt? Are you shot?'

Anatoly drifted briefly back to consciousness. He ran his arms down, slowly checking his legs.

'I think I'm OK ... just a bang on the head.'

'But we heard a shot?' Zhanna insisted.

We cleared the rest of the ice away.

'She pulled the gun on me … and we fought,' Anatoly mumbled weakly. 'I think the bullet hit her.'

At that point we were distracted by a strange noise. Muffled. About twenty metres away. Over to our right, at the far end of the crevasse.

An arm punched clear of the compacted snow.

'Viking!' Zhanna cried.

We left Kami with Anatoly and kicked our way across the face.

Viking was partly buried. Struggling to break free. Only one arm and the side of her head were visible. Blood was seeping from a ragged hole in her arm. A bullet wound.

Her breathing was rapid and desperate.

Zhanna looked at me, uncertain. She stepped away to return to her father, but I moved to block her.

'We can't leave her,' I said. 'No matter who she is and what she's done.'

Raw humanity meant we must do our best to save her.

'Zhanna?'

'I don't know.'

'Will you help me?'

For several seconds she remained still, staring into the

clouds. Then she spoke.

'You're right,' she said, quietly. 'We have to save her, if we can.'

We turned to Viking.

Zhanna swept ice away from the terror leader's face.

'We're going to try and get you out,' I said.

Zhanna began to dig.

I joined her, ramming the axe deep into the debris, trying to get a fix on how hard the ice was.

'My legs,' Viking gasped. 'Pain … '

Zhanna flashed me a look. If Viking had a serious injury it would be nearly impossible to get her down.

A hissing noise reached us. Spindrift coming down the face. We ducked instinctively, spicules of ice chilling us to the bone.

A blast of wind rocked us.

We returned to the task of digging Viking out. Ten more minutes. The top part of her body was free. The bullet wound had stopped bleeding as the blood coagulated, but it was clear she was in serious trouble.

Viking began to cry. It was strange to see such a hard character breaking up before our eyes. I felt a pang of compassion. A series of great spasms wracked her body as she sobbed deep and hard.

The bitter wind was still blowing. The tears were freezing on her cheeks.

'It's hopeless,' Viking said. 'I'm beyond help.'

We kept working, excavating Viking blow by blow from the clutches of the ice. She kept crying, great gasps that racked her body.

The ice was harder around her legs. She was still firmly entombed. We kept digging, throwing the chunks of ice down the face.

'We have to try and pull her out,' I said.

We grabbed her underneath her arms and pulled. Viking screamed, agony in her eyes.

'One more go,' Zhanna said. We worked in unison, pulled and lifted again, extracted Viking from the grip of the ice, dragging her on to the flat terrain of the small balcony. She howled with pain as we dragged her. Straight away we could see terrible damage to the lower part of her body.

'Broken … ' Viking whispered. 'My legs are broken, yes?'

I nodded. Zhanna turned her head away.

Viking's eyes became clouded. A terrible expression of utter resignation swept across her face.

'Then there's nothing that can help me,' she said.

'I'm sorry,' Zhanna said. She made to walk away but Viking stretched out her hand and grasped her by the wrist.

The Russian girl looked to me, uncertain.

'You tried to save me,' Viking whispered, 'even after all I've done.'

She licked her lips. 'Have you got water?' she asked.

'I'll give you some juice,' Zhanna said.

She poured the liquid from her flask and held the cup to Viking's mouth. She sipped it, coughing a little as the fluid caught in her throat.

The three of us were silent for long moments. Zhanna and I looked over to Anatoly and Kami, relieved when Kami gave us the thumbs up.

'He's coming round,' Kami called. Zhanna turned, ready to walk back to her father.

Viking reached out once more, holding her back.

'There's something I need to tell you, Zhanna,' she whispered. 'A secret.'

Zhanna frowned. 'Really?' she said.

She crouched by Viking, listening intently.

Viking's Story

'Many years ago I worked with your father,' Viking said. 'I travelled to Moscow to join his publicity team. For a while we worked side by side, then things changed and we became a couple.'

Zhanna's eyes widened.

'He never told you that, did he?' Viking said. She coughed, struggling for breath.

The Russian girl shook her head.

'I was young and out for fun. He was already one of the wealthiest men in Russia. I loved the private jets and the VIP rooms at the clubs. Our photos were in the gossip magazines almost every week. We travelled together whenever Anatoly had business. Tokyo, London, Los Angeles; we were masters of the universe and it seemed like anything was possible.'

Viking paused to sip some more drink. Her eyes never left Zhanna.

'He gave me a top job in the company, running public relations. That's when the rot began to set in. I began to see the dark side of Anatoly's mining operations, the damage they caused to the environment. It was my job to lie about it. He got angry when I questioned the ethics behind what he was doing. For Anatoly, everything was about profit. Nothing other than profit.'

I saw Zhanna's cheeks redden.

'We argued. It got quite vicious. I was emotional and … '

Viking paused as a wave of pain engulfed her. Her hands clutched at Zhanna, the knuckles white with tension.

' … and I was pregnant with Anatoly's child.'

Zhanna gasped. Her eyes flickered to mine.

'I gave birth to a beautiful baby daughter. I wanted to keep her but Anatoly had other ideas. He wanted to have her for himself and for me to walk away.'

I saw a great tremor of emotion pass through Zhanna.

'He always said that money could buy anything,' Viking said. 'And he really meant it. I turned down a million. I turned down five. But when he offered me ten million dollars to turn my back on my own child, I finally agreed.'

Zhanna put her hand to her mouth, her eyes wide with horror.

'I signed a contract agreeing to cut all links with my own daughter. I signed away my right to be your mother so Anatoly could get me out of his life.'

Viking paused as a coughing fit hit her.

'I let you down, Zhanna. And I want you to know how sorry I am.'

Zhanna's eyes welled up.

'I did it for a reason,' Viking whispered. 'I did it because it gave me the money I needed to set up an eco-movement of my own. To right the world's wrongs. I vowed I would destroy Anatoly's company one way or another.'

'He was cunning,' Viking continued. 'He had powerful friends in the media, in political circles. He could mount damage limitation against everything I publicised; kill the stories before they did him reputational harm.'

'When he started mining the ocean floor I knew the game had changed for the worse, but even I couldn't have predicted just how bad it would be. He has changed the climate of Asia – that's undeniable.'

Zhanna gave Viking some more juice from her flask. I helped her to sit up so she could drink it.

'Leave me,' Viking said. 'I know what I have to do.'

She moved her good hand to the pocket of her wind suit.

There was no need for conversation. All three of us understood that there was no hope for Viking. With both legs broken, only a helicopter rescue could save her, or an army of Sherpas to attempt a stretcher rescue.

Neither was available. And in any case, she was way too high for a helicopter to attempt a medevac.

'Let me stay with her a few more moments,' Zhanna said.

Her face looked different, somehow she no longer seemed like a young girl.

I kicked back across the ice to join Kami. Anatoly was gradually recovering from his concussion. The two of us helped him to sit up.

He looked over to Zhanna and Viking, talking intently at the other end of the crevasse, his eyes registering firstly confusion, then alarm.

'What is Zhanna doing?' he mumbled. 'What are they saying?'

'Viking has told her everything,' I said.

Anatoly drew his breath in sharply.

'No … ' he whispered. 'Not that.'

Minutes later Zhanna climbed up to our position. She walked to her father and crouched down next to him.

Her cry competed against the rumble of the strengthening wind.

'Is it true … ?' Zhanna began.

Anatoly put his hand around her shoulders.

'We will talk later,' he said softly.

A shot split the air.

We spun around and saw Viking's body, slumped back.

Her outstretched arm still gripped the pistol.

'I hate this place!' Zhanna cried. 'I hate Everest. I hate this place!'

CHAPTER 12

Kami pulled out a flask of drink.

We cradled cups of hot chocolate in our hands, comforted by its sweetness. Zhanna was calmer now but deep shock was still smouldering in her eyes. The revelation from Viking had been so unexpected. Her death so sudden.

After a while, Kami spoke.

'You know what this means, don't you?' he said.

'What?'

'It's over. We can go back down, to Base Camp.'

'Thank God!' Anatoly said. 'I don't think I would have had the strength to go any higher.'

Zhanna said nothing. The events of the day had taken her to a place beyond words.

I stared up at the summit. Foreshortened by the angle, it looked tantalisingly close. Close enough to touch, even if it was two full days of climbing away. For a moment I let my imagination soar up those crystal slopes, savouring how it would feel to …

I felt Kami's stare on me.

'What are you thinking?' he said.

I snapped out of my daydream.

'Oh, nothing,' I answered. 'Just wondering if I will ever get this high again.'

Kami sighed.

'I know how you feel,' he said gently. 'It looks beautiful up there. But Shreeya … the baby … '

'Yes,' I nodded. 'We'll have to save these dreams for another time.'

'We should radio the girls,' Kami said. 'They need to know we're coming down.'

We activated the radio and put out the call. Within minutes we heard Tashi's voice on the line.

'Everything's changed,' I told her. 'The Viking problem has been solved and we're free to descend. We'll come down as fast as we can.'

'That's wonderful!' Tashi broke into a delighted peal of laughter at the news. 'Wait, Shreeya wants to speak to Kami.'

Kami took the handset, talking warmly to Shreeya in Nepali for some moments, his face wreathed in smiles. Then he frowned, his eyes clouding over as the mood of the conversation changed.

The tone of Shreeya's voice shifted. She was speaking urgently and with great conviction.

Kami was shaking his head and interjecting with the occasional word.

'What's happening?' Zhanna mouthed at me.

I shrugged. I couldn't imagine what could cause Kami and Shreeya to be stressed with one another.

Then, to my surprise, Kami's smile returned. 'OK,' he told Shreeya in English. 'I understand and I accept. I see the beauty in the plan.'

He handed me the radio.

'Shreeya wants to talk to you,' he said.

'Ryan?'

'Hi.'

'I've told Kami he's not coming back.'

I felt a gust of wind race across the face.

'*What?*'

'Not until he's placed the shrine bell on the summit.'

Kami laughed at the expression on my face.

'Seriously?'

'It is written,' she continued. 'Destiny. You must go with him and say that prayer on the top of the world. Then bury the shrine bell and bring Kami back safely for me. Will you do that?'

I felt a lump growing in my throat. How typical of Shreeya to suggest something so selfless, particularly when she had to be counting the minutes until Kami could be back with her.

I looked at Kami, but I didn't need to ask his feelings, I could see the joy in his eyes.

'What do you think?' Shreeya asked.

'Can I speak to Tashi, please?' I replied.

I heard the crackle as the walkie-talkie was passed over.

'Hey, Tashi. What do you think about this crazy plan?'

'I'm totally cool with it,' she replied. 'You have to end your Everest obsession somehow, right? But I need you to take care, you hear? Don't take any mad risks.'

'OK.' I felt the back of my neck prickle with excitement.

'My love goes with you,' Tashi said. 'The gods will protect you both, have no doubt.'

Emotion welled up inside me as Kami took back the radio.

The conversation continued for a few more moments, then Kami said goodbye.

Zhanna got to her feet, throwing her arms around Kami then hugging me too.

'It's a perfect plan,' she said. 'You deserve the chance to try for the summit. Me and Papa will be OK going back alone.'

Anatoly nodded. 'It's fine with me. Viking's men will not fight on without her.'

Kami took out the shrine bell, gazing at it with great reverence.

'So the story continues,' Kami said quietly. 'The shrine bell has a destiny to fulfil.'

I stared up at Everest. That enigmatic mystery of a mountain. I had the feeling that the last piece of an extraordinary jigsaw had just fallen into place. As always, the highest ridge was alive with ice crystals, that ever-moving shroud, flowing ceaselessly with the caress of the wind. I thought of the shrine bell, guarded safely in Kami's pocket, and of what it would mean to Kami to get that bell to the top.

And what it would mean to me too. To reach the summit. For real. It was a dream beyond imagining.

'Let's finish this,' I said. 'Once and for all.'

I felt a new wave of energy pulse through me. Things had changed now. It was no longer about escape. No longer about running for our lives.

Kami and I could focus in a more personal way. For Kami, a more spiritual way.

It was about fulfilment. The completion of a dream we both shared. Long minutes passed. We stared down the valley, where the tents of Camp 2 could just be seen, nestled against the rock wall.

'OK,' Anatoly said. 'It is decided.'

He rose groggily to his feet.

We embraced our two friends one last time, wishing them speed on their descent.

I felt a pang of guilt to be leaving them. But this was our moment, Kami's and mine.

Shortly after we had begun to climb we heard a terrible cry. We turned to look down the slope, seeing that Zhanna had fallen suddenly to her knees. For a few seconds she was still. Then she threw her head back and screamed. The cry merged with the sound of the rising wind, echoing off the walls of Lhotse and Everest.

Anatoly stood near her, motionless, holding back, his head bent.

Zhanna sobbed for a while. Kami and I watched, both wondering if she would be able to get to her feet again.

I flexed my fingers inside my gloves, trying to keep them from freezing.

Finally Zhanna rose, shakily. Anatoly put his arms round her shoulders and the two of them began to descend once more.

'She's moving OK,' Kami said. 'Let's go.'

We climbed on, ever higher on the Lhotse Face, glad of the oxygen feeding into our masks. Both of us had cranked our flow rates up to four litres a minute, aware that we needed a boost on this second climb of the day.

Finding the best route was difficult. The avalanche had swept away all the waymarkers along with the top layer of snow and ice. We were climbing mostly on bare rock, our metal crampons clattering and scraping as we moved awkwardly upwards.

The wind was in a skittish mood. Like spirits playing a game. Chasing one way, then another. Not strong enough to be threatening, but breaking our rhythm and forcing us to pause during the more violent gusts.

Rockfall kept us alert, pebbles and fist-sized stones whirring down the face almost continually from great heights.

'The mountain is restless,' Kami said. 'But no more avalanche for now.'

We kept an eye on Zhanna and Anatoly. By mid-afternoon they were just two dots, almost 1,500 vertical metres beneath us.

'They've reached the end of the fixed ropes,' Kami observed.

I took the lead on the next section, counting off twenty steps before each rest, bending over my ice axe, gulping in air from the mask and wishing there was more.

It was gradually sinking in: the momentous decision we had made, the danger still ahead.

Everything felt different.

But the risks were still real.

We crossed out of the avalanche strike path. Back on to the slippery, loose ice and snow. Fixed ropes began to appear and we clipped on gratefully, happy for the illusion of safety.

Four o'clock came and went. Then five.

Knee and hip joints began to ache with a dull, insistent pain. My body was protesting at this incessant fight against gravity, every sinew and muscle joining in with complaints of their own as we crawled through a gully of deep snow.

We dragged ourselves wearily up the Geneva Spur, arms and legs like chunks of lead. As the final rays of daylight faded we hit the col, returning in silence to the tent. I collected ice and we began the process of melting it down for tea.

The endless mission to rehydrate our bodies began. Porridge laced with copious amounts of honey was the only thing we could bear to eat.

We ate in silence, thinking of our families and loved ones. Thinking of Zhanna and Anatoly who, we hoped, would be safely down in Camp 2.

In a few hours the real test would begin.

Summit day.

'Let's sort out the oxygen,' Kami suggested. We spent a busy hour making sure that our bottles were fully charged, checking that the feed line to the masks really did connect to the thread.

Without the extra gas we would have no chance of the summit.

As I busied myself, my body felt like I was hooked up to an adrenaline drip, a potent mixture of excitement and dread running through me.

A voice kept chanting in my head.

Summit day. Summit day. Summit day.

It was thrilling. And chilling. So many things could go wrong. We couldn't afford to make even the tiniest mistake.

As soon as the cooker was turned off, the temperature inside the tent fell to freezing and below. Bundled up in my sleeping bag, I shone my head torch at the canvas and watched, fascinated, as tiny crystals of hoar frost formed on the Dacron of the tent interior.

Our breath was freezing instantly as it left our bodies.

We had no thermometer to measure the extreme cold that night. My guess is it must have been thirty degrees below freezing outside. Maybe twenty below inside the tent.

We resolved to leave at midnight after a couple of hours' sleep. I tossed and turned in my bag, too hyper to switch off.

Kami was definitely snug. He was out for the count as soon as his head went down.

I thought about Tashi as the gentle sound of Kami's snores filled the tent. She would be so happy if we made it to the summit.

I smiled as I thought about all the good times we had shared at the refugee camp, feeling a strong surge of emotion. The higher we got on the mountain the more I seemed to miss her.

Kami suddenly awoke. He sat bolt upright with a great gasp of fear.

'Nightmare?'

'Yes.'

I switched on the head torch and saw that his eyes were wide. He unscrewed his water bottle to take a big gulp of juice, then fell back on to his sleeping bag, moaning softly.

'The avalanche?' I asked.

He nodded.

'Always. I get the same dream every few days. The sensation of being buried, deep beneath the snow. Unable to move. Unable to cry for help.'

We were silent for a while.

'I won't sleep again,' he said finally. 'Why don't we get ready?'

We brewed up a final litre of water for our flasks then took our time to kit up. Thermals, climbing trousers, shirts. Inner shell of fleece. Outer shell of Gore-Tex. Full-body down suit. Pertex wind suit on top.

Then the socks. Three layers. The plastic barrier to stop sweat freezing. The inner boots. Outer boot shell. The neoprene gaiter. Crampons checked and ready to snap into place as soon as we left the tent.

Head torch. Spare batteries. Camera. Swiss army knife. Energy bars. A couple of high-calorie gels.

Walking out across the col was an emotional moment for me. To think that we were treading in the footsteps of

Everest's greatest climbers, of Edmund Hillary and Tenzing Norgay, Reinhold Messner and Junko Tabei.

My spirits soared with the thought that this day might see us reach the top of the world.

'Don't have any fear, Ryan,' Kami told me with conviction. 'Everything will work out for us today. The shrine bell will take care of us.'

His words were comforting, but I was still dreading the long hours of darkness, the disorientating effect of climbing with just a tiny pool of head torch light to rely on.

The first steps sent tremors of hot pain through my legs. Our bodies had rested too well and our muscles were not remotely interested in more punishment.

'We need to pace ourselves,' Kami said. 'There's a long way to go.'

Too right, I thought.

We passed the last of the tents. Hit the rocky terrain leading towards the ridge. Doubts flooded into my mind like invading demons.

Would my body fail at this last hurdle?

Did I have the technical skills to surmount the razor-sharp precipice of the final ridge?

Would two bottles of oxygen be enough to get us to the summit?

I stared at the dark, brooding shoulder of the mighty West Ridge.

How about Kami? Was he hiding damage from his slip in the Icefall? Would his newly rehabilitated spine stand up to the challenge of this, the ultimate climb?

It would have been reassuring to have others on the skyline above us, other lights we could follow, removing the pressure of route finding from our situation.

But of course there was no one there.

We were totally dependent on ourselves. Just the two of us. A very intimidating thought.

The snow conditions were poor; fresh snow had fallen on the ridge the previous evening, and we were wading through heavy powder, taking turns to break trail.

Half an hour for Kami. Half an hour for me. Step-by-step progress, crazily slow, stepping up high to push through the metre-deep snow.

Waymarkers loomed out of the darkness. A red pennant, attached to a bamboo wand, the colour muted by darkness. The ripped-up remains of a discarded tent.

A strangely shaped mound of snow, which I suspected was a covered-over corpse.

'We are not the only ones up here,' Kami said, as he stared at the bump in the ridgeline. He had made the same bleak conclusion as me.

Another hour went by, the gradient continuously sharpening, the steepening terrain meaning every single step cost a fraction more effort than the previous one.

The broad swathe of the shoulder became narrower as we gained height, gradually funnelling down into a sharp ridge, which offered little room for error.

I thought of Tashi, wondering where and how she was. I thought about the descent we would make back through the Western Cwm and the Icefall – still a long and risky journey. We could so easily run out of time, energy and resources after our summit climb.

Without help we could be twenty-four hours from death. Just one factor – like running out of oxygen – would be enough to finish us.

When it came to the weather it was pot luck. The only tools we had were the ones that nature had given us – the ability to judge the complicated play of wind, cloud and snow by eye and by instinct.

On a normal expedition, science would have been on our side. We would have had accurate weather forecasts, satellite data coming in from meteo stations in Europe and the USA.

We had none of that.

'We're like the early explorers,' Kami said. 'Looking at the sky to see if a storm is on the way.'

Distant thunder rumbled away to the south. I closed my mind to the implications of this. This window of good weather had to last.

Several hours passed. We had reached the Balcony, a famous landmark on this classic route. On any other mountain it would hardly be noticed, just a flattish area of level terrain about twice the size of the average dining table.

On Everest's final ridge, every single step is taken on a seventy-degree incline; this scrap of even ground was an irresistible invitation to take a rest.

Kami flopped down on the ice, his head forward, resting on his knees.

'My eyesight is starting to feel weird,' he said faintly. 'Black and fuzzy round the edges.'

I unclipped his rucksack and checked the gauge on his oxygen bottle. It was reading one third full.

'Your oxygen line might be frozen,' I told him. Tashi and I had had similar problems on the northern side the previous year.

Tunnel vision is a sure-fire sign of an oxygen problem. The optic nerve shuts down when a breathing tube gets blocked with ice.

I pinched the rubber line that ran to Kami's mask. There was a hard plug of ice inside. Frozen condensation from his breath. I squeezed the line then flexed it gently until I heard the ice crackle inside as it broke up.

'That's better!' Kami said. 'I can feel it flowing again.'

Ten minutes later his vision had improved.

'You OK to keep going?'

'Of course,' he replied. Kami's raw courage was beginning to show.

The night went well, fuelled by adrenaline, physical effort and the gentle hiss of the oxygen as it entered our masks.

Just after daybreak we hit the final ridge.

The two of us celebrated by cracking open our flask and pouring out some hot tea. The warm drink gave us a welcome boost and we followed it with some mint cake, pure compacted sugar that zapped energy straight into our bodies.

We spent a while staring to the south, enchanted by the awesome cluster of mighty peaks that now lay beneath our position.

Faint streaks of light heralded the dawn. The inky black sky of night yielded to delicate pastels of orange and red.

With every passing minute we could see further and better into the valleys that surrounded us.

'Lhotse is lower than us!' Kami said.

It was true. The fourth highest mountain in the world was now beneath us.

'Let's go,' Kami said. He stood upright, striking his boots with his ice axe a few times to remove the balled-up snow that had collected in his crampons.

Kami was always the first of us to want to keep climbing. The summit was luring him on with irresistible force.

I think the turbulence that Nepal was experiencing had acted as a trigger, firing up an even greater desire to reach the top.

'Imagine the stories you will be able to tell your child,' I said.

Kami turned to me in surprise.

'That's exactly what I was thinking,' he said.

Our minds were working in perfect synchronicity.

Dawn became day. The sun quickly gained in power, forcing us to rummage in our packs for our goggles.

Half an hour without eye protection up here would be enough to give us snow blindness.

High above our position, streaky clouds were starting to form. A sign of changing weather.

The Hillary Step loomed into view. I stared at it apprehensively, this much-feared obstacle, arguably the most famous cliff in the world.

From where I was looking it seemed pretty hardcore. Jagged, fractured rock, six or seven metres high. A natural flaw in the ridge, a last gateway on the seemingly endless journey to Everest's summit.

A sting in the tail. A postscript. A final test.

'I heard it had collapsed in the earthquake,' I said. 'Got easier.'

'Wishful thinking,' Kami replied. 'If anything, it looks harder than the last time I was here.'

A ragtag bunch of ropes had been fixed up the rocky face. Even from a distance of fifty metres I could see it was a mess. Old ropes are dangerous, they can snap without warning.

We would have to treat it with utmost respect. We couldn't afford to make the slightest mistake.

The route took us along the knife-edge of the mighty ridge, vertigo-inducing drops to our left. Our ice axes were essential here, especially on the frequent sections where no fixed ropes were in place. The crunching sound of axes thrust into ice became a reassuring background noise.

We were resting every five or six steps, legs deadened

with fatigue, minds numbed with the repetitive nature of the challenge.

Kami was showing signs of exhaustion. Once or twice I saw him swaying uncertainly, as if he were half asleep on his feet.

My mind slipped into a hazy kind of dream state for a while, snapping back to attention when I realised that the awkward-looking chimney in front of me was the Hillary Step we had seen from afar.

'Choose the red rope,' Kami said. His expert eye had picked the best of a very bad bunch. The scrappy protection, on which we were relying, had been there for a full year and was questionable to say the least.

'Someone's got to go first,' Kami said.

'I'll do it.'

I slid my jumar clamp up the line, feeling it bite with satisfying precision. Trusting it with my weight, I pulled hard with both arms, at the same time kicking higher into the compacted ice at the side of the Hillary Step.

I tried not to think what would happen if the snow anchor failed. A fall down the 2,000-plus-metre South-West Face of Everest was not an attractive prospect.

Half a body length of height gained. Two lungfuls of air expelled and replaced at high speed. I paused there, sucking in precious oxygen from the mask as a glittering parade of white stars raced around my view of the world.

'Slowly,' Kami warned.

I took another lunge up the rope. My foothold crumbled as the ice fractured, sending one leg skittering down. I shifted my weight to the other leg, praying the crampons would remain in position. I pushed the jumar up higher. The rope became taut.

Almost there. The bulging snow hump at the top of the step was an arm's length higher.

I had another pause. Sucking on the gas mask, wishing I had thought to crank up the gauge to a higher rate of flow for this section.

Down on the ridge I could see something buried, something breaking the smooth outline of the snow. Behind Kami. Blue fabric. It looked like an arm, a shoulder. The rounded shape of a head.

I shivered. Another Everest victim.

A body in the ice.

'I'm freezing!' Kami yelled. 'Get a move on, Ryan.'

My right arm went up, pushing the jumar up the final metre of rope. I kicked into the ice, tested the strength of the foothold and pushed upwards.

I belly-flopped on to the top of the cliff, squirming on

my front for a few seconds before crawling to the flat ice that lay just beyond. I rested for a couple of minutes then went back to the lip and saw Kami preparing to climb.

Lying prone, I rested for five minutes while Kami fought his way up the fixed rope. I could hear the grunts and explosions of breath that it involved. I should have helped to pull him up the last exhausting section but I was still trying to recapture my breath.

Kami crawled over to my side, flopping down with a dramatic sigh.

'That's the biggest challenge over,' I said.

'Don't assume anything,' Kami replied, coughing as he laughed. 'You know what happened to me last time.'

I looked along the ridge.

The summit was in sight. We were on the final section of the climb. My heart, already working overtime to pump super-oxygenated blood, tripped with the raw excitement of the moment.

'The summit pole!' I yelled at Kami. He stumbled up the snow step and, breathing incredibly hard, put his hand on my shoulder.

'Can you see it?'

He nodded back, too exhausted – too emotional – to speak.

I bit my frozen lip.

We were going to do it. What could stop us now?

I felt Kami coming closer. He pulled down his oxygen mask. I heard the cracking sound of ripping ice. Small chunks of frozen condensation fell off his mask as he spoke.

'This is where it happened,' he told me. 'Where Alex turned me around.'

I stared at the ridge, mentally measuring the time it would take to reach the summit. Half an hour? Perhaps a bit more? I was astounded at how close Kami had got on his previous expedition.

'Heartbreaking,' I said.

'Totally,' he agreed.

It was crazily close to the summit to turn around and yet I could understand it. There is a limit to what the human body can take. A strict and unbreakable ceiling to what it can ultimately endure.

The mind can take you beyond. Desire can help you to push further than you ever dreamed. But, as Alex Brennan found that time, the human body is a machine; you can take it so far but finally it must stop.

At that moment I was close to the limit myself.

But I still had something left.

We crouched down in a small hollow, pouring hot tea

from the flask. The fluid was life itself, the warmth spreading deliciously, restoring vital heat to our frozen body cores.

We were now in an incredibly exposed place, the highest mountain ridge on the planet, so it was hardly surprising that the wind came back to taunt us. It began with a few tentative gusts, then steadily increased over the next twenty minutes to become something more threatening.

'We could do with some fixed ropes here,' Kami yelled at me.

There were none. We dropped a few steps down the windward side of the ridge as we continued, hyperaware of the overhanging cornices that could so easily lure us too close to the Kangshung Face.

Many climbers had been killed by that small but fatal error. I could see all too clearly how easy it would be.

I was worried about Kami but he showed no signs that the wind was troubling him. He just kept going with that slow but determined step.

To our right, the clouds were gathering. Thick masses of them. Dark and brooding.

Everest was a magnet for bad weather, particularly late in the day. If there was a storm front around, it would inevitably hone in on the mountain sooner or later.

That was why so many Everest climbers had been caught

out on their return. Afternoon storms striking when the body and mind were at their weakest point.

Now the summit was tantalisingly close. Close enough I could make out the individual colours of the prayer flags that were flapping there. Close enough that I could finally believe nothing could stop us.

Three more steps. Breathe hard. Three more steps. Breathe again.

My mind was foggy from the lack of oxygen. My body racked with the pain of the climb. Yet, somehow, I was still able to enter the zone, keeping that crucial one-step-at-a-time mentality alive inside me.

Kami came up alongside me during one of my rests.

'Be cool if the two of us reached the top at the same moment,' he said.

'It sure would,' I replied.

CHAPTER 13

The ridge was wide enough for us to walk side by side. The steep ground fell away, becoming a series of gentle undulations in the final fifty metres.

I was still trying to shake my brain out of its altitude-induced haze. Like many mountaineers before me, I found I was talking to myself in a way that felt completely normal.

You are about to step on to the summit of Mount Everest, I told myself sternly, the 'voice' in my head as clear to me as if it had come from another person. *This moment will happen once in your lifetime. You have to appreciate it to the max. Open your eyes and drink it all in.*

I stepped up and placed my hand on the summit pole. Kami held back a bit, I guessed he was searching for the shrine bell in his pack.

I forced myself to concentrate. I couldn't let the emotions take over completely. I wanted to be able to tell Tashi everything about this moment. I couldn't share it with her for real but I could bring it alive for her through my words and memories later on.

I fixed it all in my mind. Every crease in the clouds. Every gust of wind. The fluted snow folds of the sinuous ridge we had just climbed. The tatty prayer flags draped in such glorious confusion about the summit pole.

Then came Kami.

The ice collecting on his mask. His piercing dark eyes shining through the lens, the tiny crystals of frozen tears on his wind-scorched cheeks.

I reached out and gripped his shoulder. He bent his head and I sensed he was praying.

What a roller-coaster ride it had been for him. Paralysed in an avalanche, resurrected by medical science. There were no words for what he must be feeling at this moment.

It was too deep.

Kami. His eyes glowing with the incredible light of pure joy.

He brought out the shrine bell. It looked tiny cradled in his climbing mitts, light glinting off its polished surface.

'Third time lucky,' he said.

'The Dalai Lama will be pleased.'

'Join me for a prayer,' Kami said.

Kami said his prayer in English for my benefit. We bowed our heads into the wind.

'*Whoever so much as sees this sacred place,*' Kami said, '*will feel a spontaneous surge of vivid faith.*

'*Here is where groups of countless devas throng,*

'*And Buddhas proclaim their dragons' roar of perfect wisdom. A sublime space in which disciples see the truth. A scene of wonders, and a scene of marvels.*

'*A blessed site to which the bodhisattvas flock,*

So that they might hear the perfect teachings.

'*Through the virtue of praising this outstanding place, may we travel without obstruction to the Buddha's realm.*'

He rang the bell to tell the gods the ceremony was over. The tone was clear and sweet, even above the blustering rumble of the wind.

'I will leave the bell here,' Kami said. 'It will make my prayer more powerful.'

'This is where it belongs,' I agreed.

We chose a spot about a metre from the summit pole. Taking our ice axes, we chipped away at the ice until we had dug a hole deep enough.

'This bell was a gift from the gods,' Kami said. 'Now it is time for it to be returned.'

As Kami placed the shrine bell into its resting place a powerful clap of thunder rang out to the south. We turned, looking into a wall of solid cloud spiked with flashes of lightning.

I was fearful, but to my surprise, Kami laughed.

'You know what that is, don't you?' he said.

His mouth widened into a smile, his face filled with serene joy.

'A storm?'

'It's the monsoon, Ryan! The monsoon!' he cried.

'What?' My hypoxic mind took a while to catch up with what he was saying.

'Those clouds have come from the Indian Ocean. That's the front of the weather system Nepal has been waiting for.'

I stared at the approaching mass, realising he could be right. It didn't seem to be an ordinary weather system; the clouds were darker than any Himalayan storm I had ever seen.

'Clouds filled with rain,' Kami said. He was laughing now. 'This year the rice will grow. This year the people will not starve. The shrine bell has worked its magic.'

'Seriously?'

I found myself laughing with Kami. It seemed crazy to me that he believed his prayer could bring about the monsoon, but the fact that he believed it was undeniable.

To Kami there were no limits to what faith could achieve. I put my arm round his shoulder and hugged him tight.

'Your prayer seemed to work pretty quickly,' I told him.

Kami beamed in delight.

We buried the shrine bell in the hole, scooping in chips of ice and packing them down tight with our gloved hands.

Soon it was lost to sight.

'We need to take some photos,' I said.

I pulled out my camera and we took it in turns to take shots of each other. Kami raised his ice axe above his head, copying the summit pose Tenzing Norgay had struck in his first ascent of the mountain. Then we took a selfie of the two of us with the summit pole in the background.

'Take a last look,' Kami said. 'I don't think we will ever see anything so beautiful again.'

I let my eyes drink in the view, the rumbling clouds to the south, so elemental and filled with power. The hazy brown plateau of Tibet to the north, mysterious and seemingly infinite in scale. I took a close-up photo of my hand on the summit pole and packed the camera away safely.

'Our mission is complete,' Kami said with satisfaction.

'Not quite,' I told him. 'There's still the descent.'

Kami smiled.

'I think it will be fine,' he said.

We turned, heading for the fixed ropes that would lead us down.

Journey's End

CHAPTER 14

Kathmandu was quiet. The rains had changed the mood in a positive way. The riots and protests had died away for the moment. An uneasy calm had taken over from violence and demonstration.

There was still no government in place. Basic needs like a water supply and electricity were sporadic and liable to fail every day.

On the positive side, there were fewer people living in the streets. Many thousands of Nepalis had returned to their villages and farms on the arrival of the rains. They were now planting to take advantage of the monsoon. Hoping for a bumper rice crop to fill hungry bellies and start earning cash once more.

The aid agencies had closed their food kitchens.

My reunion with Tashi was extra sweet. And Shreeya was delighted to be back with Kami. We shared a hundred stories, swapping tales from the mountain for their adventures escaping down the glacier.

Anatoly and Zhanna were also recovering in the city and we spent an emotional evening with them, learning about their journey back. As we had suspected, Viking's men had cut their losses when Operation Killer Storm fell apart, and headed off into the hills with their loot. Nevertheless, the terrorist attack had shaken Anatoly to the core and armed guards now permanently surrounded him and Zhanna.

Dawa, who was as cool as ever, had been reunited with Anisa and they had both been given their jobs back. We could never forget how he had saved us back in the Icefall.

We said our farewells to the Russians. Anatoly was sincere as he thanked us for our help on the mountain.

'Come and stay on the yacht sometime,' he offered. We made some vague comments about how great that would be, but everyone knew it would never happen.

Tashi and I took it in turns to give Zhanna a huge hug.

'I will never forget Everest,' Zhanna said. 'I'm sure I will think of it every day for the rest of my life.'

'Do you think you'll ever go back?' Tashi asked.

Zhanna's smile faded, the memory of her mother's confession clearly on her mind.

'I think not,' she said. 'Too many ghosts … '

Zhanna and her father flew out of Kathmandu for Moscow in the biggest private jet I had ever seen.

Alex's death haunted us.

We felt like we had abandoned him up there in the Icefall.

Finally, we got some money together and paid a Sherpa team to retrieve Alex's body from the ice. His remains were portaged down to Lukla and flown to Kathmandu where we held a special ceremony to celebrate his life.

One thousand butter lamps were lit in the temple of Annapurna, right in the heart of Kathmandu's old town. Hundreds of mourners were present, including members of Alex's family and many of his friends from the States.

Following the ceremony, Alex was cremated on the banks of the Bagmati River. There, amidst the dust, and beneath the outstretched wings of red kites using the heat of the funeral pyre as a thermal high in the air, Alex Brennan's journey ended.

In accordance with local customs, his ashes were swept into the river.

The siege at Base Camp had ignited a new wave of global media interest in Everest. Journalists had flown into Nepal in search of survivors; a television crew was talking about doing a reconstruction for a documentary.

Five of Viking's men were eventually apprehended, living wild in the mountains in a valley about thirty miles from Everest. They were placed in custody awaiting trial, but since Nepal's justice system was inactive, there was no telling how long their detention would be.

They had looted vast amounts from Base Camp, stealing cash and valuables from the tents and more than 200 passports. The possessions were gradually being returned to the mountaineers who had lost them, but the process was slow and inefficient.

No one was weeping any tears on their behalf. They were a mercenary force of the worst kind, renegade soldiers who had defected from the armies of other nations and been seduced by Viking's promise of big money.

They were killers and crooks.

They could rot in jail forever as far as we were concerned.

I thought a lot about Everest in the days that followed.

We had climbed it. But did Kami and I really *know* the mountain?

Could anyone ever *know* it, as such?

Probably not. Everest is never the same mountain two days in a row. Minute by minute she rises, forced upwards by the tectonic forces playing beneath our feet. Continents are colliding below the earth's crust, building stress, thrusting an entire mountain range into the sky and stretching it across a massive swathe of the planet.

Everest doesn't just rise. She also changes, shrugging off layers of ice and rock in an ever-flowing series of unpredictable events. Earthquakes shake the highest slopes, sending rocks that have been in place for millennia crashing into the valleys. Cornices of ice form with the clamouring wind, defying gravity for a while before they succumb.

Even the innocent snowflake, fluttering down on to Everest's slopes, can work sinister magic with trillions of its sisters, sending avalanches to cut short the dreams of the strongest men and women.

Tashi agreed to come back to the UK with me. I was planning to spend a couple of years working on my parents'

farm and then make a new application to study at uni. We returned to the refugee centre to say an emotional goodbye, taking leave of the many Tibetans we had grown to know and love during our volunteer year in the camp.

'We will return next year,' Tashi told them. 'Work in the holidays.'

The airport was back in business. As the riots had eased off, international flights had begun to return to Nepal.

Kami and Shreeya came to say goodbye.

'You must send us a photo as soon as the baby is born,' Tashi said.

'For sure,' Kami said. 'You'll be the first to know.'

'Come to England when you can,' I urged Kami. 'The mountains aren't quite Everest but we can still have some fun in Scotland.'

'Yes, we'll apply for a visa as soon as the baby is old enough,' he said.

Kami embraced me, hugging me hard.

'My Everest brother,' he said. 'We have been touched by the gods.'

'I couldn't have done it without you,' I said.

Kami gave me that world-expanding smile of his. The smile that lifted all who saw it.

'Keep believing, Ryan,' he said. 'Believe in the power of

the universe. Believe in yourself.'

'I will,' I told him. 'Everest has given me faith.'

Kami and Shreeya walked us to departures, waving and smiling right to the final moment as we went around the barrier and lost them to view.

One hour later we were on board the flight. The plane was half full and we could choose our seats.

'You can have the window,' Tashi told me with a smile.

I took my place. The aircraft taxied out to the runway and took off into the prevailing, easterly wind. We began to climb, the captain's voice crackling through the intercom as we gained height.

'Ladies and gentlemen, boys and girls, those of you on the left-hand side of the aircraft might like to know there is a good view of Everest as we climb out of the valley.'

Tashi and I smiled.

'I just had the strangest sense of déjà vu,' I told her.

We stared out of the window and there she was.

Everest. Illuminated brilliantly in the early morning sun, standing proud of the clouds that swarmed around her base. Nothing came close to her sheer intoxicating beauty; she was, in every sense, the ultimate mountain.

I thought about Kami's incredible achievement. Overcoming his paralysis and then climbing Everest. If ever there was a demonstration of the power of prayer and raw determination, then Kami was it. In a very real sense, he had been reborn. He had risen from the shell of a shattered body and achieved a feat that takes the human body to the limit.

It brought a lump to my throat. To gaze on the summit. To think that I too had stood on that highest and holiest of places was almost too much for my mind to cope with. I had left England two years earlier looking for adventure, but never imagining for a moment just how extreme that adventure would become.

And how much Everest would come to mean to me.

Had Everest changed me? Probably, yes. But it would take a while for me to find out exactly how.

'There's your route,' Tashi said. Her head was jammed next to mine, drinking in the vision with just as much enthusiasm.

We could see the whole of the Lhotse Face, the flatter terrain of the South Col, looking ridiculously small at this enormous distance. There was a substantial amount of snow on the range. Everest was completely cloaked, the camps all invisible, buried deep.

'How long do you think the shrine bell will stay on the top?' Tashi asked.

'For ever, I hope,' I replied. 'Or at least long enough for Kami's prayers to take effect.'

'It will be there for years,' she said. 'That should do the trick.'

The aircraft began to bank, circling in a great loop as it turned towards the west.

I craned my neck, watching the mountain until the very last moment.

Then it was gone.

Tashi curled her fingers into mine. Her head rested on my shoulder.

I gently pulled the window blind down.

It was time to go home.

END OF THE
EVEREST FILES TRILOGY

WITH THANKS TO ...

This is the end of a long journey and there are plenty of people to thank.

The Sheffield-based climbing company Jagged Globe ran the logistics for the two Everest expeditions I joined for research purposes in 2016 and 2017. Thanks to Simon Lowe, Tom Briggs and Stephanie Hopkinson for setting things up so well and to David Hamilton, Dick Gale and Andrew Todd for their competent and inspiring leadership on the hill. Personal thanks also to Matthew Bartlett for joining me on the second trip and Chongma Pemba Sherpa for guiding me so pleasantly to Camp 2.

I ran several student focus groups during the drafting stage of the book. It is always useful to get critical feedback and the story changed in some interesting ways and was improved greatly by the students' comments.

At King James's School in Knaresborough, Librarian Lisa Bryden and Assistant Librarian Susie Chapman gave copies of the second draft to pupils Phoebe Carmichael,

Tabitha Gibson, Millie Jones, Anna Liptrott, Hannah Lee, Alex Owen-Hughes, Esme Slater, Arthur Watson, Ellie Wilson, Sam Wilson and Jess Whittaker. Their analysis was very useful indeed.

Duke of Kent School has also participated enthusiastically in my focus groups and given excellent feedback under the guidance of teachers Tom Southee and Katharine Brookes; thanks to Lexi Botting, James Ebers, Guy Rudman and Siena Taylor for their response.

Cara Keyman at the excellent Robert College in Istanbul also set up a focus group amongst the pupils. Their comments were brilliant and I would like to thank Beril Babatürk, Ayda Çolakoğlu, Ata Engin, Azra Haseki, Yiğit Kılıçoğlu, Zeynep Kızmaz, Serra Koçoğlu, Elifnaz Önder, Yağmur Öztürk, Selin Pınarer, Lara Sakarya, Melis Sezginel, Sezen Zeynep Sümer and Deniz Yağmur Ürey for reading and reporting on an early draft.

At Shrine Bell and Vertebrate Publishing, Camilla Barnard, Jon Barton, Jane Beagley, John Coefield, Lorna Hargreaves, Nathan Ryder and Susie Ryder and have been hugely supportive throughout the Everest Files adventure. Thanks team V, you have, as ever, done a great job – as did Sarah Darby with the excellent chapter heading illustrations that have accompanied each of the books in the series.

My heartfelt thanks also to Alice Williams and Marco Zadnik, and finally to my fellow author Ruth Eastham for being the perfect travelling companion on this long and exciting journey.

ABOUT THE AUTHOR

Matt Dickinson is an award-winning writer and filmmaker with a passion for climbing and adventure. During his filmmaking career he has worked as a director/cameraman for National Geographic television, the Discovery channel, the BBC and Channel 4. His film projects have taken him to Antarctica, Africa and the Himalaya, often in the company of the world's leading climbers and expeditioners. His most notable film success was *Summit Fever*, in which he reached the summit of Everest via the treacherous North Face. His book *The Death Zone* tells the true story of that ascent and has become a bestseller in many different countries.

Matt is currently patron of reading at Eltham College and continues to climb and explore. In January 2013 he summited Mount Aconcagua, which, at 6,965 metres, is the highest peak in the world outside the Himalaya. In 2016, and again in 2017, he was back on Everest as a writer in residence with Jagged Globe's South Col Expedition. Currently, he is planning an ascent of Denali in Alaska, one of the 'seven summits'.

Recently Matt has started writing fiction for teenage readers. His debut thriller series Mortal Chaos was well received by critics and readers alike. Matt has followed this up with the Everest Files, a dramatic and popular trilogy set on the world's highest mountain. *Lie Kill Walk Away* is his latest teen thriller. Matt tours the UK, speaking at schools and colleges and inspiring a new generation of adventurers.

Fascinated by Everest?
Want to know more about the world's highest peak?

The Everest Files website is packed full of fascinating facts and features.

- Find out about Everest, the Himalaya and the effect global warming is having on the area. Geographical facts with study guides for teachers.
- Watch the summit footage taken by the Everest Files author Matt Dickinson after his epic North Face ascent.
- Discover more about the Sherpa people and their way of life.
- See an interview with Jordan Romero, the thirteen-year-old boy who became the youngest person ever to summit Everest.
- Learn more about the Everest Files trilogy, including a video message from author Matt Dickinson.

If you would like an author visit from Matt Dickinson for your school or club, contact details can be found on the website.

www.everestfiles.com